SHADOW CHASER

D0029885

OTHER BOOKS IN
THE SON OF ANGELS: JONAH STONE SERIES

Spirit Fighter

Fire Prophet

SHADOW CHASER

Son of Angels
JONAH STONE

Book 3

JEREL LAW

THOMAS NELSON
Since 1798

NASHVILLE   DALLAS   MEXICO CITY   RIO DE JANEIRO

Published in Nashville, Tennessee, by Tommy Nelson. Tommy Nelson is a registered trademark of Thomas Nelson, Inc.

Cover illustration by William Graf, © 2013 by Thomas Nelson, Inc.

Tommy Nelson titles may be purchased in bulk for educational, business, fund-raising, or sales promotional use. For information, please e-mail SpecialMarkets@ThomasNelson.com.

Library of Congress Cataloging-in-Publication Data

Law, Jerel.
   Shadow chaser / Jerel Law.
      pages cm. — (Son of angels ; book 3)
   Summary: "Jonah's story comes to resemble a modern-day Job as he's faced with trials that affect his health, strength, relationships, and most-prized possessions. As he and the other quarterlings prepare for mid-term exams, their powers are tested once again in the most fierce battle against Abaddon's forces yet. Will Jonah's faith in Elohim continue to persevere as he fights Abaddon in his hardest battle yet?"— Provided by publisher.
   ISBN 978-1-4003-2199-5 (pbk.)
   [1. Angels—Fiction. 2. Good and evil—Fiction. 3. Faith—Fiction. 4. Christian life—Fiction.] I. Title.
   PZ7.L418365Sh 2013
   [Fic]—dc23   2012046607

Printed in the United States of America

13 14 15 16 17 18 RRD 6 5 4 3 2 1

For Christopher,
who is generous, kind-hearted,
and stronger than he yet knows.
I believe in you.

CONTENTS

CONTENTS

PART I

SHADOW AND LIGHT

Now faith is being sure of what we hope for

and certain of what we do not see.

Hebrews 11:1

ONE

An Unwelcome
Discovery

Jonah Stone was defending a New York street all by himself. Fallen angels, their wings withered and charred, swooped in, attacking him from all sides. There wasn't anyone he could call for help. He was on his own. He tried to fight them, tried to turn away or run, but he couldn't move and he couldn't look away. He was surrounded. Everywhere he looked, there was another fallen angel crawling out of a manhole, leaping from a window above, or materializing out of thin air. He looked up but saw only a crush of dark feathers there too. There was no escape.

Jonah struggled to move down the street. It was as if he were trying to pull his feet through thick sand. The harder he tried, the worse it became. His feet began to ache, a dull throb, like a feverish flu, moving up into his legs. His stomach, his arms, and all the way up his neck and into his head—everywhere he felt the aching, and it made it almost impossible for him to move.

Just when he was sure they were going to kill him, Jonah woke up, the vision shattered. He blinked a few times, reminding himself that it was just a dream. His body wasn't aching. He didn't seem to have a fever. He'd been having vivid, frightening dreams ever since the prophet Abigail had revealed to him that he was a prophet too. He breathed in and out until he felt his heart rate begin to slow again.

His eyes scanned his darkened bedroom in the convent. *These rooms sure haven't changed*, he thought. The room held the same simple wooden furniture—two beds and two desks against the wall, a worn circular rug on top of the old hardwood floor, and a small window with a view of a brick wall. It wasn't much, but it was comforting to be back in his familiar room after two weeks in Greece.

Jonah looked around for his roommate, David, the only quarterling taller than him, but he wasn't there. His bed was already neatly made, and he was probably down at breakfast. David and his sister, Ruth, were from Uganda, where their parents ran an orphanage for hundreds of kids. David knew as much about the Bible as anyone Jonah knew, including his sister Eliza.

Jonah hadn't known there were others like him, other than Eliza and his brother Jeremiah, until they'd rescued their kidnapped mother from underneath the dark New York City streets. After all, they *were* what they were because of her. She was a nephilim—her mother was a human and her father was a fallen angel. When they rescued her, they also found and rescued others like her.

That was over a year ago now, though it felt more like a lifetime. Back when their eyes were just opening to the reality that there was so much more to life than what they could see, and that the darkness of the battle between Abaddon and Elohim was going on behind everything. The war between good and evil was invisible to humans, but very, very real. Fallen angels could be around any corner, ready to twist minds and hearts away from Elohim.

Last year, Jonah, Eliza, and Jeremiah had met not only the other nephilims' children, but also had begun Angel School together. Jonah still cringed when he thought about what could have happened to them all if Abaddon's recent attack on the school had been successful. Thanks to the prophet Abigail, the angels, and most of all, Elohim, they had managed to push back the evil.

His friend David had been beside him every step of the way, helping and encouraging him, especially with the realization that Jonah, too, was a prophet.

Jonah grabbed a towel, shampoo, and soap and walked down the hallway to the boys' bathroom to shower. There were three shower stalls and a sink with a mirror over it. When he emerged from the shower, he stood in front of his reflection and did a double take.

"What in the world is that?" he whispered, touching his face. There was a red spot just above his left eyebrow. He touched it and immediately wished he hadn't.

"Owww!" It was a giant zit and it hurt. He studied it in the mirror from all angles. "Well, this is just great," he muttered. He tried to pull his shock of hair down far enough to cover it, but it didn't help.

Jonah tried to shrug it off as he headed down the steps and into the dining hall. Most of the other quarterlings, with the exception of Frederick, noticeably absent, were already sitting at the long wooden table in the middle of the room, talking loudly and eating breakfast. Jonah walked over to the buffet line, grabbed a plate, and filled it with everything that caught his eye.

"Morning, guys," he said, sitting down between David and

Andre and across from Rupert and Carlo. Jeremiah was down beside Eliza and the rest of the girls, and, as usual, he had everyone around him in giggles.

"Good morning, Jonah." David smiled, taking a huge bite of biscuit.

Andre simply nodded, barely looking up from his enormously stacked plate. It truly was awe-inspiring to see the Russian eat.

"Good day, Jonah," said Rupert, glancing up at him. "Hey, what is that on your forehead?" He pointed his knife toward Jonah's face as he asked the question.

Jonah pulled at his hair a little, trying to make it drop farther onto his face. "What are you talking about? And hey, how about getting that knife out of my face?"

"Oh, sorry," Rupert said, lowering his knife but continuing to stare. "It's just . . . that's quite the spot you have there, Jonah."

David turned and studied Jonah's face too. "Wow. That's enormous!"

Andre glanced over, and when he saw it, even he stopped eating. Carlo's eyes widened, and he touched his own forehead sympathetically.

"Stop it, okay?" Jonah said, beginning to panic at the sight of four sets of eyeballs pointed at his forehead. "You guys are creeping me out. Haven't you ever had a pimple before?"

"Yes," Carlo said, swallowing a bite of pancake. "But not like that."

"Yeah," David agreed. "I've just never seen one so big. It's like Mount Kilimanjaro."

Jonah rolled his eyes and stuffed a bite of egg in his mouth so he didn't say something he might regret. His friends finally, mercifully, changed the subject to who their favorite soccer player was.

That night, just before nine o'clock, thirteen kids disappeared from sight in front of the door of the convent. All of the quarterlings had entered the hidden realm. The hidden realm, a place that humans could sense only within their hearts and souls, was a place the quarterlings could actually see and enter into. In the hidden realm, they were invisible as they walked several blocks to the New York Public Library.

The early November air was chilly. Jonah led the way, trying to keep them in the shadows as much as possible, even though the people they passed couldn't see them. He didn't want to walk through anyone—that was for sure. It was not only weird; it was shocking—literally—for everyone involved.

Mainly, though, they needed to be cautious when it came to the nonhuman elements they might encounter on the street. The city streets were always teeming with fallen angels. They had been safer when their hideout at the convent had been a secret, but the Fallen had discovered their location during their last battle. This made Jonah even more thankful for the angelic guard flying above them and the angels who walked in front of and behind them.

Jeremiah was at the front of the line and was kicking at the heels of the angel walking in front of him, trying to trip him. The winged creature kept glaring back at him as if he were angry, but Jonah saw him wink. It was hard to get mad at Jeremiah.

"You need to stop that," Eliza said, coming up behind her little brother. "What if you tripped him and caused a commotion? That much noise could attract some of the Fallen, for sure."

Jeremiah grinned up at her and kicked the angel's ankle one more time.

Eliza raised her hand and was about to punch him in the arm, but Jonah grabbed her wrist.

"Enough, guys," he said. He eyed his mischievous younger brother. "Eliza's right, Jeremiah. Settle down out here. This isn't the place to goof around."

The side door to the library had been left open, as usual. Jonah glanced around to make sure no one was watching and then slid the door open, motioning for everyone to go through quickly as he held it.

But as soon as he shut the door, he heard a scream and a dog barking. He turned, and directly in front of them, a German shepherd had cornered Hai Ling against the wall. The security guard holding the dog's leash was staring at the Chinese girl.

TWO

JONAH'S
UNCOMFORTABLE URGE

Hai Ling squealed nervously, frozen in place, as the security dog barked loudly and the security guard squinted at her. Jonah was sure the security guard couldn't actually see Hai Ling. There was no way—unless she was no longer in the hidden realm.

"Molly!" The guard tugged at his dog's leash, but she wasn't budging or quieting down. "What's gotten into you, girl? There's nothing there!"

Jonah sighed with relief. He couldn't see Hai Ling. But Hai Ling was still frozen against the wall, her eyes wide as she stared at the dog's sharp teeth.

"Hai Ling," Jonah said calmly. "The guard can't see you, and the dog can't hurt you. He just senses your presence. You know how dogs are, remember?"

But she didn't respond. She was too afraid to hear him.

Jonah walked over and stood beside her in front of the crazed dog. "See? He can't do anything to hurt you. Come on back over here with the rest of us." He reached down, grabbed her hand, and led her back over to the group. That did the trick. Shaking, but all right, Hai Ling blushed with embarrassment.

"Okay," she mumbled. "Sorry. I'm okay. Let's just go. Stop staring at me, will you?"

They walked past the guard and the dog, which was now sniffing the floor where Hai Ling had stood.

Jonah loved walking into the library. It wasn't like anything they had back in Peacefield. The super-high ceilings were painted in intricate detail to look like the sky. Portraits and statues lined the walls as they made their way around the corner and up a grand marble staircase.

Camilla stood at the doorway of the main reading room, welcoming them with a smile and a twinkle in her eye. It was their first night of Angel School since they had been forced to leave two weeks earlier.

"Welcome back!" she said as they filed in. "From all the way around the world, we are once again here together. Come in, come in."

As usual, the enormous room was empty. Wooden desks with reading lamps sat in clumps throughout the room, which was bigger than a football field.

Three other angels stood in the middle of the floor.

"Marcus! Taryn! Samuel!" Eliza shouted, running over to greet them. She gave Taryn a hug. Taryn stroked her hair and smiled.

"It's good to see you again too, dear Eliza." The warrior angel smiled, her red hair brushing against Eliza's face.

"We haven't seen you since . . . since . . ." Eliza stopped. The image of them being defeated by fallen angels during their last battle was still fresh.

Jonah stepped forward, high-fiving Marcus. "We knew you weren't dead or anything—not that you could die—but we missed you."

"Believe me, friends, those fallen will come to regret the day they tried to destroy us," Marcus said. He was smiling, but he still managed to look determined.

He winked at Jonah, then turned to chat with Andre, who was waiting eagerly to show Marcus how much his strength had improved. Jonah looked around and watched as his friends greeted their favorite teachers. He felt incredibly blessed to have them all on his team.

"Samuel, I've missed you and our class discussions," said David, slightly bowing to the thin-necked angel holding an old Bible in his hands.

Samuel bowed lower. "And I have missed your tremendous insight, young David. I've missed every one of you."

"So where is everybody?" The voice came from behind them as a young preacher with a goatee and long dark hair rounded the corner. "It's time to get this thing started again."

"Quarterlings," said Camilla. "Why don't you greet Reverend Bashir yourselves?"

They nodded, then bowed together, praying for Elohim to allow them to exit the hidden realm. They suddenly appeared in front of the Pakistani pastor.

"Wow! It's like watching popcorn pop!" he said, taking them all in. "I never get tired of that. How are all of my friends? It's been too long."

They rushed to greet him, with Hai Ling leading the way,

suddenly all giggles and smiles around their handsome, human instructor.

"Okay, students," Camilla said, calling their attention back toward her. "You can go ahead and reenter the hidden realm now. There is no need to risk being seen by anyone else. Of course, as usual, you will reappear when studying the spiritual arts with our dear friend here." The students reentered the hidden realm as she continued. "Tonight, Angel School is back in session!"

The quarterlings clapped. Jonah found himself getting more and more excited. He wanted to grow in his skills as part angel, but he also wanted to find out as much as he could about what it meant to be a prophet. He was hoping to find some assistance from the instructors.

"You will remember that during your previous school session, you were matched up with others who possess similar gifts to your own," she said. "We will continue with these same groups. But you have advanced in your learning, and now there will be additional things to discover. You are no longer beginners on this journey. You are expected to apply everything you have learned, both from the classroom and in battle."

Camilla prayed for Elohim's blessing on their Angel School session and that He would help the quarterlings understand and use their gifts. But mostly she prayed for His presence to be felt and remembered among them, and for His protection. With one eye cracked, Jonah peeked up at Camilla as she prayed, her hands raised in the air. The familiar tendrils of light, only visible in the hidden realm, were there, twirling from her shoulders and head, rising up through the library ceiling as her prayer circled its way to Elohim.

As she continued to pray, though, Jonah began to feel

something in his stomach. It started as an uneasiness—a gurgling, even—that made him place his hand there. *Maybe it was something I ate for dinner,* he thought, *and it just isn't sitting well.* But the sensation seemed to grow into something that encompassed more than his stomach alone.

Was he about to get sick right in the middle of a prayer? Jonah inadvertently raised his hand to cover his mouth. He really didn't want to throw up in front of everyone.

But even though something was welling up inside of him, this felt somehow different. Something was coming up. The hand he had placed over his mouth wasn't going to stop it. Jonah looked to the right and left for the nearest bathroom or escape route.

His feet wouldn't do what he wanted them to, though. In fact, they began to move him forward until he was in front of the quarterlings, instead of away like he wanted. He stopped right next to Camilla, who was still praying.

She glanced up, distracted by his footsteps toward her, and her eyes grew wide. She paused mid-sentence.

Jonah's cheeks felt as if they were about to explode. *Keep it down, Jonah,* he told himself. *Keep it down! What are you doing up here? Whatever you do, don't open your mouth!*

But the urge was too great. He looked around at the bowed heads of the quarterlings, wild-eyed. He was going to vomit on the floor of the New York Public Library.

How embarrassing.

He squinted his eyes and gritted his teeth with one last effort of defiance, but there was no stopping it. When his mouth opened, though, only words poured forth. He raised his hands in the air, and suddenly a calmness washed over him as he gave himself over to what was inside him.

"Friends," he said, with power in his voice that caused every quarterling to snap to attention. "Don't be foolish—Abaddon is still lurking, prowling around like a lion, waiting to trap us. His Fallen are plotting to destroy us, even now. Be strong in Elohim, and trust Him. Also, trust one another. A dark day is coming . . . in that time, you will have to find your strength in Him or you will not find it at all."

Jonah closed his mouth and lowered his hands, and felt a deep sense of relief. He was pretty sure that the message had come from Elohim Himself.

He was lost in his own thoughts for a few seconds, unaware of anyone else in the room. *What a rush.*

Then he looked up again and remembered where he was. Twelve faces stared at him—plus the three angels.

"I . . . uh . . . ," he muttered, running his fingers through his matted hair. "Sorry to interrupt." He had gone from momentary elation to awkward discomfort in a matter of seconds.

Camilla regained control, but she was watching Jonah carefully as she spoke. "Okay, quarterlings," she said, clapping her hands and snapping everyone back to attention. "It's time to head to your classes for the evening."

Jonah began to slink off toward Angelic Combat with Marcus and Taryn.

"Jonah, just a word, please?" Camilla said, stopping him in his tracks.

He sighed, bracing himself for more humiliation. The blood had already rushed to his face.

Camilla folded her arms, studying him. "What was that, dear?"

Jonah shrugged his shoulders, unable to look her in the eye. "I don't know . . . it just kind of . . . happened. Like I couldn't hold it in, and if I did, I was going to explode."

"Yes, yes," she said, nodding slowly. "It's your prophetic gift, coming to life."

"Seriously?" he asked. It had felt like the words were coming from Elohim. It was a relief to know he wasn't going crazy. "Well, I'll make sure I don't let it interrupt again."

"No, no, you mustn't say things like that," she said, drawing nearer. "It is textbook prophecy. You are given something to say, and no matter what, you have to say it. It is the blessing of being a prophet."

"Yeah, well, it feels more like a curse," Jonah said, blushing. "I mean, it's kind of embarrassing."

She smiled. "Maybe the right word is a *burden*. But remember, speaking the words of Elohim is never a curse—and it's certainly not embarrassing. Be proud that Elohim chooses to spread His messages through you." Camilla's eyes were drawn to Jonah's forehead, and she frowned.

"What is that?"

He had forgotten all about the massive pimple on his face until then.

"Ugh," he said, realizing that he had just been standing in front of everyone with the huge blemish in full view. "It's just a zit. I don't suppose you have any special angelic zit cream, do you?"

"Afraid not, dear," she said, brushing the hair off his face gently. "It does look awfully . . . painful."

Jonah pulled back before she could touch it. "It is," he said. "It popped up this morning. I'm sure it will be better tomorrow."

She stared at it a little longer, and it was impossible for him to tell what she was thinking. Breathing in, she seemed to want to say something but then thought better of it.

"On your way, Jonah," she said softly, ushering him to class. Jonah walked over toward Marcus and Taryn, glancing back at Camilla as he felt her eyes upon him still.

THREE

SOLITUDE

When Jonah joined David, Frederick, Hai Ling, and Lania in Angelic Combat, Marcus was in the middle of a demonstration on firing arrows while running.

"And so, what you want to do is continue moving your feet, focus on your target, pull your arrow like so"—he moved across the center of the room, an arrow appearing in his fingers—"aim, and . . . fire!" Marcus was at almost a full sprint as he aimed at the target across the room. He dove as he released the arrow, falling down behind an overturned table. It pierced the red bull's-eye he had posted against the wall, then disintegrated as it touched the special paper they used for target practice.

"Nice shot!" David said as he and Lania clapped loudly. Frederick and Hai Ling continued to stand with their hands in their pockets, but they nodded. It was an impressive shot by any standard.

"Thank you for the demonstration, Marcus," said Taryn, turning to the five quarterlings. "As you experienced in your battle here in New York, you don't often get to shoot an arrow when you are standing still."

"Too bad we can't have a suit of armor made out of that angel paper," commented Frederick. "That would be kind of nice in battle, don't you think?"

Taryn smiled. "Too bad it only extinguishes our arrows, Frederick. Not those of the Fallen."

They began to practice shooting while they moved. Marcus had made it look easy, but all of them struggled to even come close to the small target on the wall. *At least I'm not the only one having a hard time with this*, thought Jonah. Even Frederick, who usually excelled in archery, had a tough time getting used to shooting on the move. All of their arrows continued blasting into the wall around the target.

Jonah did his best, and he was glad to be back in training, but he felt rusty and distracted. His mind kept wandering back to his outburst of prophecy. Just thinking about it made him feel a little queasy. It had been uncontrollable. He also noticed how the others—even David—were watching him when they thought he wasn't looking. Were they staring at him because of what he'd said or because of the giant zit on his forehead?

He touched it gently. It seemed to be growing.

And what was worse, it felt like another one was starting to emerge on his cheek.

None of his arrows came even close to the target.

"We'll try again tomorrow," said a tight-lipped Taryn, who did not seem happy with their performance. "But I would suggest you all work a little harder on your focus."

Jonah's group's next class was Scriptural Studies with the angel Samuel. They sat down at the other end of the large room, which had been arranged with two tables and chairs. There was an ornate podium in the front where Samuel stood, wings folded behind him, his neck craning over the large book. He barely noticed when the students sat down in front of him.

"Oh . . . when did you all get here?" he said, finally looking up from his book. "Well then, let's begin."

A stack of Bibles and notebooks was on each table, along with a cup full of black pens. Jonah pulled one of each toward him and waited for Samuel to begin.

The skinny-necked angel had what must have been a few hundred papers strewn across the podium. He searched through them intently, some of them falling on the floor, which he ignored. There were a few scrolls there too. He opened up one of them, frowned, and then opened another, frowning again.

"Do you need some help, Instructor Samuel?" asked Lania. She bent down and picked up the handful of papers he had dropped.

"Thank you, dear, thank you," he said. His eyes grew brighter as he held up one of the papers in his hand. "Aha! There they are: class notes!"

He thrust himself into a lecture about Abraham, the father of the Israelite people. He spoke with passion about the time Elohim called Abraham to follow Him and told him that He was sending him to the Promised Land. But Elohim only told Abraham to get up and leave, not telling him exactly where to go.

"Imagine the faith it took to say, 'All right, I'll go!'" Samuel exclaimed. "'I don't know where You're telling me to go, but I'll take the first step!'"

Jonah had heard that story, and the others Samuel told about Abraham, like about putting his son Isaac on the altar as a sacrifice, dozens of times. But he had never heard them come alive like this. He found himself captivated by the old stories, as if he were listening to someone who had witnessed these things firsthand. *Samuel probably did see these things with his own eyes*, he reminded himself.

One other student didn't seem quite as enthralled as the rest, though. After forty-five minutes in which Samuel had barely caught his breath, Frederick raised his hand impatiently.

"I'm sorry, but where is all of this going?" he asked bluntly, looking around at the others. "Is this going to have a point anytime soon?"

Jonah glared at him, as did the others. It was typical Frederick—rude and arrogant. Even though he had given his heart over to Elohim at the end of the battle last year, the old Frederick still came out pretty often.

Samuel was undaunted, however. "Behind all of our study is a purpose and a plan, my friend Frederick. Even if you cannot see it at the moment. It's not unlike life," he said, looking up above them as he spoke. "You never know how what you're doing in the present is going to influence the future. Elohim has a plan, but He works in unexpected, mysterious ways."

"Well, it just seems like—"

"Enough!" Samuel snapped, grabbing the podium. His papers went flying onto the floor again, and Lania scrambled to help him pick them up. Frederick shut his mouth but snickered to himself.

Jonah thought about Samuel's words. He wasn't sure he fully grasped what Samuel was getting at, but something inside of him agreed.

He lingered after class, fidgeting with his notebook until he was the only one who hadn't moved to the Spiritual Arts class with Reverend Bashir.

Samuel looked up from shifting his papers around. "Ah, Jonah. How are you, my son?"

Jonah stood up from the table and approached the wise angel. "I am not quite sure how to ask this . . . but I'm just wondering about the prophets in the Bible."

Samuel looked at Jonah, and his eyes began to dance. "Studying the prophets could consume a lifetime, and much, much more. There is a lot to learn from them."

Jonah nodded. He knew that he probably needed to dig into them more in his reading. "I just . . . it feels weird. I'm supposedly, well, according to Abigail, at least, one of them." He hesitated to even call himself the word. "She said that I'm a prophet."

"And if your statement a little while ago to the students is any indication," Samuel observed, "then indeed, you have the gift."

Jonah shrugged, nodding as he stared at his own shoes.

Samuel moved from around his podium and placed a gentle hand on his shoulder. "Jonah, I know it's difficult for you to accept and understand. I can imagine it makes you feel different from the others. I have no help to offer you there. All of the prophets in the Bible felt that way. It was part of their burden, what they had to carry. But I can tell you," he said, squeezing him firmly and making sure he caught Jonah's eyes, "that it is a gift with great honor. And consequence. You must learn as much as you can about it and embrace it."

Jonah thanked him, knowing it was time to get to his next class. He left Samuel, though, with more questions than answers, his mind stirred up once again by the thought of somehow being different from the rest.

He exited the hidden realm and caught up to the rest of the kids making their way toward the Spiritual Arts classroom. The

Pakistani-born pastor greeted them at the door, smiling easily, dressed in jeans and a simple white T-shirt.

"It's great to see you again, friends," he said as they took their seats in a circle in the small stone-walled room. A friend of the convent and the pastor of a big New York City church, Reverend Bashir had been invited in last year to teach Spiritual Arts. Jonah had no idea at the time how powerful these ancient practices could be. Prayer, after all, was something he thought only pastors or older people in the church did. How wrong he had been. "You guys look great, and all of you look older. And taller. Man!"

"We are quarterlings, you know," said Jonah. "We grow taller a little faster than normal."

He smiled at Jonah and then began. "I want to remind you that the Spiritual Arts are not simply for your own personal growth. They are a battle tool, just as much as fighting with arrows and swords," he said, pointing toward the door. "I'm sure you remember the power of your prayer, and those of the sisters in the convent, against the fallen angels."

How could they forget? An entire wall of protection had formed all around them, based on prayer alone. None of them, not even Frederick, could take prayer for granted anymore.

"There are other practices that are just as powerful," he said, sitting down in the circle with them, resting his elbows on his knees as he leaned forward. "We will be studying and practicing them together this year. They are designed to connect you more deeply with Elohim and help you fight the battle. One of them is called *solitude*."

He launched into a lecture on the practice of solitude. He described it as a listening kind of silence. According to Reverend Bashir, solitude was different from prayer because solitude was about hearing, not speaking. The more the pastor explained, the less comfortable Jonah became. He didn't particularly like being left alone to his own thoughts.

But that was what Reverend Bashir was instructing them to do, and soon, Jonah found himself with an assignment—go find a quiet place in the library and spend the next fifteen minutes being perfectly still.

Just. Listening.

The quarterlings looked at the reverend uncertainly but filed out of the room.

"Remember," he called out to them as they left, "reenter the hidden realm. And all you have to do is focus on Elohim and listen."

Jonah looked at David, shrugged his shoulders, and walked down the empty hallway to the right. He was back in the hidden realm and didn't worry about being spotted by anyone. The place was deserted anyway.

He found a set of steps, wandered down them to the floor below, and sat down on the cold marble floor in the corner of a hallway. Jonah tried to get himself to be quiet and still, but it was harder than he realized. His eyes darted around, looking at the pictures on the wall, a scrap of paper on the floor, a statue of the head of some bearded man . . . When it was quiet, everything seemed to try to get his attention.

Jonah sighed, closing his eyes, and emptied his thoughts, listening.

What could he hear? His breathing was slowing gradually. His heartbeat drummed in his ears. The rush of air from a vent nearby whooshed gently.

He strained to hear more deeply. Was anything there? Any

voice other than his own, echoing around in his head? He had just spoken the words of Elohim to everyone, and yet now he couldn't hear a thing.

He cheered silently when the time for this exercise was up and he was able to return to the classroom.

"How did it go, everyone?" Reverend Bashir asked.

To Jonah's surprise, several of the others had something to share. Lania had heard the word *trust* and David had heard *I am your comfort*—even Frederick shared about his mind going back to the mountains of South Africa, where he grew up, and how he finally saw that this beauty was from Elohim alone.

Jonah sat quietly, shifting his feet on the dusty floor. He had nothing to say.

"Remember," their instructor said, "it's not always about what you hear. Solitude is about being quiet and letting what happens happen."

Jonah couldn't help but think that what had happened was that he had wasted fifteen minutes of his life listening to the building creak.

FOUR

A Special Guest

The next two weeks of Angel School were much the same, filled with evenings of practicing the spiritual arts, listening to lectures, and honing their combat skills. After all of that, and keeping up with their regular schoolwork, the quarterlings didn't have a lot of free time left over.

But every spare minute Jonah could find, he spent in the convent's library, reading about the prophets. Even though Jonah had never been accused of being a big reader, he tore through every book he could find, taking notes in a small notebook.

So far he had learned a lot, and none of it was very comforting. Prophets were often picked on, singled out, and misunderstood. People sometimes even tried to kill them. But they all seemed to be so focused on speaking the words of Elohim that they ignored everything else.

As Jonah realized this, he looked up from his books and stared for a while at the brick wall in front of him, sighing loudly. How was he ever supposed to be like that? He always cared what people thought. He genuinely did want to learn more about prophets, but his other reason for hiding out in the library was to avoid the others. His one pimple had turned into dozens, and his face was covered in oozing zits.

It was hard to actively listen for Elohim's voice when Frederick's filled up his ears all the time. He had taken to calling Jonah names in front of everyone else. The others didn't join in, but most of them laughed, except of course for Eliza, Jeremiah, David, and Julia, Eliza's Brazilian roommate.

It was either, "Hey, pimple-face!" or "How's it going today, ProActiv?" Or the classic, "What's up, pizza-face?" Frederick would laugh at how funny he was, and it was all Jonah could do not to unleash all of his angel strength on the boy. His friends stood up for him, especially Eliza. But it was still embarrassing. He knew the giant zits were gross.

It wasn't like he hadn't been trying to do something about it. He had made more trips than he could count down the street to the Duane Reade pharmacy, trying every cream, lotion, and pimple cleanser they had on the shelves. None of them worked. He was even beginning to think they were just making it worse.

One afternoon, Jonah secretly made a trip back down to the Chinatown area of the city. There were all kinds of places that offered herbal remedies, mostly run by shrunken, ancient-looking old women. Maybe one of them could help.

He picked a shop and opened a creaky old door, immediately finding himself in a space that was probably one-quarter the size of his dorm room back at the convent. Its shelves were lined from top to bottom with jars. He tried not to look too closely at any of them after noticing that one contained chicken feet suspended in brown goo—it was disgusting.

The shop's owner was there behind the counter and wasted no time helping him.

"Ah, pimple-face!" she said, pointing at the blemishes.

Jonah sighed. *You too?* He put his hand up to cover his face out of instinct. "I was wondering if you might have something that could help me, you know . . . with these."

She hopped up from her stool and found her glasses. Grabbing a small wooden ladder, she peered upward until she spotted the right jar.

"There it is," she murmured, putting the ladder carefully against the shelf and climbing up. She came back down with a small brown jar in her hand.

When she opened it, the smell slapped Jonah in the face like a fly swatter. He backed up, the awful smell filling the room. He glanced at the door, feeling like he was about to gag. Apparently, however, the lady was immune to the scent.

She took a pair of chopsticks and pulled out something slimy and flat, placing it in her hand. Jonah held his nose but stepped forward, peering down in horror at the triangular, skin-like object.

She held it up toward his forehead. He pulled away again.

"No, no!" she said. "You must do this! Make it better."

You asked for this, Jonah, he said to himself, closing his eyes and leaning down.

She ripped off a piece of tape from beside the register, and whatever it was, he felt her taping it to his forehead.

"There! Now it get better," she said, leaning back and admiring her work. She had taped the mystery item to his head. He was beginning to feel light-headed. "You leave on for rest of day, and bad pimples disappear. You see."

Jonah reached upward to touch it.

"No, no!" she said, grabbing his arm. "You no touch! Leave, okay?"

Jonah relented. "Okay," he mumbled. "What exactly is it?"

She was returning the jar to the shelf. "Baby hog ear," she said with a wave of her hand. "Soaked in black ink of giant squid. Very rare."

That alone was enough to make him almost lose his breakfast on the shop floor. But he willed himself to leave it on. *I'll just avoid everyone for the rest of the day, and then this thing will be gone.*

He paid the woman and left the shop, stopping for a minute to study his reflection in a shop window. It pretty much looked like he expected—a pig ear taped to his head.

Jonah felt the stares of people on the street, but he kept telling himself that it would all be worth it if the hog ear worked. He rode the subway with his head hanging down, trying to pull his hair over the pig ear. Soon after he sat down, though, several people had covered their noses and moved to other places in the car.

Jonah, on the other hand, was starting to get used to the fumes. *It's not so bad*, he kept repeating to himself.

He exited the subway as fast as he could and headed up the steps to street level. Just as he was climbing up, though, another group of kids was coming down.

"Jonah?"

Jonah glanced up and found himself face-to-face with Rupert, on the landing in the middle of the flight of steps. He was with Andre, Frederick, Hai Ling, and Bridget, one of the Austailian quarterlings.

"What's that on your forehead, Jonah?" Andre asked, staring at the pig ear.

Jonah looked down, pulling his hair over his forehead again. "Nothing. Just . . . a bandage."

All of them leaned in closer, backing him into a corner as they studied it.

"Ew!" Hai Ling said, stepping away as she held her nose. "What is that *smell*? Is that . . . *you*, Jonah?"

"I'm not sure," Frederick said, holding his nose as he studied Jonah's head, "but it appears to be some kind of . . . animal part. Jonah?"

Jonah pushed him out of the way and took the steps two at a time. "Leave me alone, all right?!"

He got out of there as quickly as he could, but not before he heard their cackling laughter chasing him down the street.

When he finally took off the baby hog ear, after wearing it the rest of the day and hiding in his room, the zit actually seemed worse.

"It didn't work," he muttered, staring into the mirror.

He showered three times, just to be sure he got rid of the smell, and joined the others for dinner.

After they had eaten huge plates of steaming fried chicken and mashed potatoes, Camilla strode through the door, her enormous silver wings sparkling, and Jonah was immediately grateful for the distraction from his forehead. At her side was another angel, one he had never seen before. He was taller than her, with a chiseled face and long blond hair that fell below his shoulders. When he moved, his red cloak shifted back and forth, like flames in a fire.

Camilla was speaking to him in hushed tones. Jonah strained to hear what they were saying, but he couldn't make anything out.

The angel nodded a few times, let his eyes dance around the room for a few minutes, and then walked back out, with Camilla following close behind.

"Who do you think that was with Camilla?" asked Julia as they began to turn their attention back to their meal again. "He looked kind of important."

Eliza pulled out a huge book that had been sitting in the chair next to her. The leather binding was cracked and weathered. She set it down on the table, dust flying off the ancient tome.

Jonah grew curious and walked over, standing behind her chair. He studied the cover and the scrolled printing on it.

"*Mortimer's Guide to Angelic Creatures*," Jonah read. "Wow, Eliza. Where did you get that book?"

She glanced up at him through her glasses. "From the library downstairs, of course. Where else do you think I'd find something like this? Barnes & Noble?"

Eliza opened the book and began to talk faster. "I took it back to my room last night and have been studying it a little bit. I was going to return it this morning. It's fascinating reading. This Mortimer guy is an angel himself, according to the author bio here. He wrote this book about all of the famous angels Elohim created."

She fingered the second page in, containing a description of the angel and a picture, which almost looked three-dimensional. An angel sat in a chair, wings spread behind him. He was holding a book in one hand and a writing instrument in the other. The description read:

Mortimer, servant of the most high God, created by Him and for His pleasure, serving under His will and direction, forever. It is my great honor to record these pictures and short biographies of those who have been made to serve Him and be enjoyed by Him. The following are short summaries of the more notable beings in the angelic realm. While every angel is important, these are those who have played prominent roles in the history of humankind. To Elohim be glory forever and ever!

"He reminds me of Samuel," Jonah said, studying his picture. Their instructor for Biblical Studies was a brilliant angel who made the material come alive, more than any teacher Jonah had ever been around. "I wonder if they know each other."

Eliza began flipping through the old pages of the book. "I recognized that angel with Camilla from thumbing through the pages last night," she said. The others had gathered behind her, watching and pointing at each page.

"Here we go! I knew I'd seen him somewhere before," she said, the pitch of her voice rising higher. She pressed down the page and held the book so they could all see.

Jonah peered over her shoulder, leaning down closely to see the lifelike image of the angel they had just seen. He stood with his hands on his hips, looking out with almost a glare, his hazel eyes seeming to point right at his. A golden angelblade was secured at his waist.

Above the picture was a set of words Jonah couldn't recognize, written in Angelic. Below that was written:

Human approximation: Nathaniel

Eliza scanned the three paragraphs written about him. "Looks like he is a colonel for the Second Battalion of Angelic Forces of the West . . . He has a long list of accomplishments in battle . . .

several 'Golden Wing' awards, apparently that's for exceptional bravery . . . It basically says he is one of Michael's right-hand men. In charge of training . . ." Her voice trailed off as she chewed on these new facts.

"Wonder what he's doing here?" Rupert asked. "Maybe he's going to be a new instructor. Think we're going to have another class now? We already have Angelic Combat, Scriptural Studies, and the Spiritual Arts . . . I couldn't stand having to learn a new subject."

Eliza shook her head. "No, I don't think he's here to be a new teacher, Rupert. Judging from his profile, that doesn't seem to be his style."

They threw around a few more ideas, but nothing seemed to stick. Jonah stood up straight again, looking back at the door. "Well, something tells me that we're going to find out why he's here pretty soon."

Hai Ling, who had been leaning against the wall and chewing on a fingernail while observing all of them quietly, spoke up. "Is that Prophet Jonah speaking, or just a hunch?"

Jonah was about to respond with a comeback of his own when, thankfully, Taryn popped her head into the room.

"We thought now would be a good opportunity for you to spend some time catching up with your parents before classes," she announced. "Join me outside on the sidewalk, and you will be able to speak to them via Angelic Vortex."

It had been a while since Jonah had spoken with his mom and dad, and like the rest, he was excited to hear from them. Maybe his mom would even have a suggestion for his skin.

A group of warrior angels was waiting for them outside. Taryn joined the Stone kids, and they huddled together close to the building. She raised her arms, and soon a tornado was swirling around them. It looked like the ones Jonah had seen on television in Kansas, except that it was perfectly quiet and didn't destroy anything.

An image of Benjamin and Eleanor Stone appeared in front of them, along the inside wall of the vortex.

They greeted their parents. "Hi, kids!" Benjamin said, waving at them, a huge smile on his bearded face. "It's so good to see you."

"Jonah, Eliza, Jeremiah," Eleanor said. "How are you doing? We miss you so much."

Jeremiah began to rapidly fill them in on all the happenings at school and in the convent. They listened as closely as they could, but soon their mom began to rub the side of her head. She leaned over to the side, out of their view, and coughed.

Eliza picked up on it immediately. "Are you doing okay, Mom? You don't look so good."

Eleanor spent several seconds trying to clear her throat. "Yes, I'm fine, dear," she said. "Just haven't been feeling all that well lately. Half of the congregation has this nasty cold going around."

Benjamin patted her on the back. "She's in good hands here," he said. "So, Jonah and Eliza, how are things with Angel School?"

After another few minutes, Taryn cleared her throat. "It's time to go," said Taryn. And before Jonah could ask them if they had any suggestions for his pimples, they were gone, the vortex disintegrating around them with one final rush of air.

"Mom didn't look too good," Eliza commented to Jonah as they watched the others finish their conversations. "Kind of pale."

"Yeah, I guess so," said Jonah. "I'm sure Dad is taking good care of her."

Frederick walked past them toward the convent doors.

"Where's the thing on your face, Jonah? What was it, like, a pig ear or something?"

He laughed as he kept walking.

"What's he talking about?" Eliza said, hands on her hips.

Jonah turned to go. "Nothing."

After Angel School, all of the quarterlings gathered back in the main reading room of the library for some final words from Camilla. Before class had begun, she had said there would be a special announcement tonight. There were whispers in the hallway between the students.

"What do you think this is all about?"

"Maybe someone is getting a new angelic power!"

"I hope we're getting a new place to stay. Our rooms are horribly small."

Jonah didn't think it was either of those things, though. Camilla stood before them, and then another angel walked out from the shadows.

"Friends, we have a special guest with us today," she said. "I want you to meet one of the commanders of the Second Battalion of the Angelic Forces of the West. He is a lieutenant colonel. You may call him Nathaniel."

A blond-haired angel stood in front of them as if he were chiseled out of granite and nodded at them without smiling. "I am here as an official representative of the Archangel Michael himself," he said, stepping forward and looking each of the quarterlings in the eye. "Sent here to observe, encourage, and provide guidance when necessary."

"Observe what?" Eliza whispered to Jonah. He shushed her.

Camilla stepped forward. "Nathaniel is here to observe your upcoming midterm examinations. These will be practical examinations to see how you use the skills you've been taught outside of the classroom. After all, it's one thing to answer a question or complete a task in here, and quite another to do it in a real-life, dangerous situation."

"And what is more," Nathaniel added, with a dramatic pause, "while I will be there for every test, the Archangel Michael himself will be present for final practical."

FIVE

QUESTIONS

Jonah looked over at Eliza, who raised her eyebrows at him. Then to David on his left, who beamed at him with anticipation. That was no surprise. Studious Eliza and David had probably both been itching for some tests for months.

Camilla stepped in. "Your midterm examinations will consist of a written portion, a skills examination, and conclude with a battle simulation."

Jonah eyed Eliza, nodding in approval, no doubt about the written exam. He wasn't so sure about that, but he liked the sound of the other two parts of the test.

"Now listen," Nathaniel spoke up, "these exercises are not simply for fun or because we have nothing else to do. They will be designed to test you, to push you to extremes, and even to simulate situations you very likely will encounter with the Fallen." He eyed them carefully before continuing. "You will be pushed to your limits, then beyond. Not only with your mental and physical skills, but within your soul as well. Make no mistake: you will experience all of your human emotions—especially fear."

Jonah couldn't help but wonder what he meant by that.

"Just know that everything that happens is with one goal in mind: to make you a better quarterling."

Nathaniel nodded to the students, bowed low to Camilla, and strode out of the room.

The quarterlings bombarded Camilla with a thousand questions. *When will it start? What should we be prepared for?* Hai Ling asked what they were supposed to wear.

Camilla tried to respond to as many of their questions as she could.

"The exams begin in one week. The written portion will take place right here. As for the skills exam and the final battle, they will be held in undisclosed locations. We want you to be prepared to fight in any sort of place, so we won't be telling you beforehand. You'll just have to adapt as you go. Let me just say I think you will find these events both inspiring and challenging."

The questions kept coming. Finally, Camilla put her hands up and said loudly, "All right, all right! My goodness, you are an inquisitive bunch for after midnight! But enough questions for now. It is time for you to be dismissed, to head back to the convent, and to have a good night's rest. Tomorrow we will begin our preparations in earnest."

They walked back in the hidden realm, but instead of their usual cautious steps, the quarterlings were rowdy, their energy feeding off the exciting news.

Jonah pressed along in silence, unlike the others. He had a lot on his mind. He felt a twinge of excitement and nerves about the exams, like the rest. But as he touched his face again, he felt yet another bump beginning to rise on his cheek. His skin really was beginning to look like a slice of pepperoni pizza!

He felt a nudge on his arm. "You okay?"

Julia's face shone up at him in the shadows of the street. He felt himself raise his hand up across his cheek to try to cover his pimpled skin from her view. He pretended to scratch his face as they walked along.

"Yeah," Jonah said. "I guess so."

"You don't have to do that, you know," she said. "Covering your cheek with your hand. I think your face looks just fine."

He lowered his hand slowly, feeling flushed, and grateful that it was dark. Her eyes lingered on his cheek, though. He could feel her stare.

"It's bad, isn't it?" he said. "It's okay, you can say it. I know that my face is breaking out."

"Well," she said slowly, "it does seem to be . . . getting worse. Maybe you should try to see a doctor . . ."

Jonah sighed, thrust his hands in his pockets, and walked forward, ahead of her. He didn't want to hear it. He had already tried the Chinese remedy, and it hadn't worked. And he didn't see how she would want to be around him looking like this anyway.

He ignored her calling out his name and kept walking along by himself.

⚭

Jonah knew something was wrong before he rolled over in bed the next morning. He felt achy and slightly chilled, but his sheets were soaking wet, like he had been sweating. When he did try to move, he felt the sheets chafe against his arm like sandpaper.

"Ahhh . . . ," he moaned.

What was more, he was having a harder time opening up his eyes than usual. His face felt large and puffy. Forcing his eyelids open, he managed to push himself off the bed and stand in front of the mirror on the back of the door.

"Oh man," Jonah said, leaning closer into the mirror. "Oh man!"

It wasn't just his face anymore—his entire body was covered with red sores. He was wearing only gym shorts and no shirt. His face still had dozens of spots, but now his chest and arms had even more. And just like the ones on his face, they were red, swollen, and painful to touch.

Jonah suddenly felt queasy. He lurched for the door and hurried down the hallway to the bathroom. He barely made it.

When his stomach mercifully stopped heaving, he sat on the floor, leaning against the cold metal wall, locked inside a stall, clutching his knees to his chest. The cold actually felt good on his back, and he held himself still, trying to gather his thoughts.

"Jonah?" a soft voice called. He could tell it was David, but he rolled his eyes and tried to ignore it.

"Jonah, I know it's you," David said. "I saw you go in there. And I kind of heard you too."

Jonah still didn't respond.

"Do you need me to go get a doctor?" his friend persisted. "Or at least one of the nuns?"

"No," Jonah said finally. His voice was barely above a whisper. "I'm . . . okay. Just some more sores."

"You're okay, huh?" Jonah heard the doubt in David's voice. "Well then, let me see."

Jonah knew David wasn't going to give in. Reluctantly, he

reached up and slid the lock open, pushing the door outward and looking up at his towering Ugandan friend.

"Oh, Jonah," David said, crouching down beside him to get a better look. He reached out his hand but must have thought better of it, drawing it back. "You look horrible. This all happened since last night?"

Jonah nodded. "I don't know what's going on. I woke up, and this is what I found." He held up his arm in front of him, counting the red splotches.

"That's some teenage outbreak," said David. He grabbed Jonah's hand and pulled him to his feet. "The only thing I know is that you really need to see a doctor. And I don't want to hear any arguing."

Jonah wasn't in the mood to argue anymore.

Sister Patricia, after looking him over with great concern, immediately sent one of the sisters to him with the urgent care facility around the corner from the convent. "At least for now," Sister Patricia had said, concern etched on her face, leaving Jonah to think that her preference was actually to send him to the hospital.

He walked out of the doctor's office a few hours later with four different prescriptions, along with a warning not to use any more Chinese remedies on his skin.

One more stop by the pharmacy, and they were heading back with a bagful of medicine—an antibiotic "for extreme cases like this," the doctor had said, plus three different types of creams and lotions. Jonah found that he also was leaving with a little more hope. He didn't even want to wait until he got home to take the pill. Stopping at a fast-food restaurant and sneaking into the bathroom, he swallowed a huge pill and began rubbing the lotions all over.

Jonah avoided the rest of the quarterlings that afternoon, but by that evening, he was hungry, and the delicious smells wafting down the hallway made his stomach growl.

He snuck into the dining hall behind David, trying as best he could to hide behind his friend. Jonah was almost as tall as him, though, and it wasn't long before he noticed Rupert lean over to Bridget and whisper something in her ear while looking in his direction.

Trying to ignore it, he picked up a plate and loaded it with lasagna, salad, and a hot garlic roll.

He sat down at the end of the table, David across from him. Eliza, who had been watching him from a distance, immediately excused herself from her friends and came to sit beside her brother.

She looked up and down his arms and at his neck and face. "You look terrible," she said, taking a bite of lasagna. "What did the doctor say?"

Jonah sighed and went through it again with her. "It's just a skin rash or an outbreak of acne or something."

Eliza raised her eyebrow at him, a cloudy look on her face. "I don't know . . . It doesn't look like any acne I've ever seen before."

"Just because you've never seen it before doesn't mean it's not normal, okay?" Jonah said.

"Yikes, sorry," she said, her face darkening. "I'm not making fun of you. I'm just trying to help."

The others slowly came over at different times during the meal to check on him. Even Frederick stopped by on his way to dump his tray.

"Wow, Stone, it's getting worse," he said. "Who would want to look like that the rest of their life?" He shrugged his shoulders and walked past him.

Jonah picked up his tray, scowled at everyone in the room,

and slammed it down a little too hard on the dirty dishes table, sending his fork and spoon flying across the floor. He collected them as everyone stared, a few of them stifling their laughter, and he bolted from the room.

But even Frederick's teasing couldn't keep Jonah from getting just a little bit excited about class. Camilla looked at him long and hard as he came in, demanding he push up his long sleeves so she could have a better view of the sores on his body. She muttered something under her breath that he couldn't hear, glanced over at Marcus and Taryn, but said nothing to him, only excusing him to go to his class.

"All of your individual angelic gifts will be tested in your exams," offered Marcus as they joined him for Angelic Warfare. "You will need every bit of your giftedness, and then some. The best thing is to be prepared for anything."

They scribbled notes furiously as Samuel told them about the written portion of the exam.

"Your written exams will begin next week," he said, looking down at his notes on his podium. David was the only one in Jonah's group who seemed to be looking forward to them. "They will cover all the areas we have already studied and the reading that has been assigned that we have not had time to cover in class."

He went on to speak so fast Jonah could barely keep up, listing most of the books of the Old Testament and the New Testament. On top of that, there were the books *Famous People in Angelic History* and *Prophets and Their Prophecies*. Jonah had scoured the prophecies book, but the other one he hadn't even opened yet.

I am in trouble, Jonah thought to himself as they left.

The next ten days were spent practicing every night, with the intensity growing each time they gathered together. The quarterlings worked on everything. Jonah ended up with mountains of note cards as he studied with Eliza and David, trying to keep up. With each card he added, Jonah felt another pound of weight added to his shoulders. They were also working harder and harder at their skills in battle and in the spiritual arts. Everything would be tested, all of their skills, culminating in the final battle simulation.

Jonah could feel the tension rising among his friends, and the competitive natures of some of the quarterlings were really starting to show. Frederick had taken to turning every conversation he could back to his skill with the bow and his powerful angel strength.

Any hope Jonah had of the medicine helping was slowly fading. He continued to apply the lotions several times a day and take the pills on schedule, but his face and arms weren't getting better. In fact, he was pretty sure the sores were multiplying exponentially. He tried to focus on the exams, but Jonah was feeling worse every day. His stomach hurt, the sores itched and stung, and his head throbbed nonstop. It made it tough to concentrate, and he felt as if he were walking around in a fog most of the time.

Two days before the midterms were to begin, he lay on his bed, staring up at the ceiling, daydreaming about acing his exams. He looked down at his arms again, and the sores that still covered them. He heard the names some of the quarterlings had begun to call him in his head. Maybe the exams would be a chance to gain some respect from his fellow quarterlings. No matter what he looked like.

SIX

A MEETING OF SHADOWS

A man in a dark business suit walked out of a prominent building, passing by the flags in front that represented the peace-seeking nations of the world. He strolled over to a street vendor, who had parked his red cart along the street. He paid for his cup of black coffee and walked across the street, taking a spot on a bench beside a set of steps leading down to the subway.

He watched the cars, buses, and cabs zoom by. His eyes were drawn to the masses of people shuffling by on the streets around him. They were rushing by, most looking either worried or depressed. He gulped the coffee, a drop dribbling down from the edge of his lip.

After a minute, he couldn't help but smile. So many of them, living meaningless lives—worried about the wrong things. Throwing their lives away.

They were lost, longing for something they knew nothing about. He slowly breathed in and reveled in this.

Another man sat beside him on the bench. He was tall and very thin, wearing old jeans with holes worn through. An old military jacket covered his gaunt body. He had gloves on his hands, except for his fingers, which poked through holes that had been cut out. A knit cap topped his knotted blond hair.

The man in the suit turned toward the other, as if just now noticing him.

"I don't suppose you have a good report for me this time?"

The man in the old jacket glanced up, making eye contact for only a second. Long enough for the other man's eyes to flash a defiant red at him before returning to brown.

"Phase one is underway and going quite well," the man reported. "The boils are all over his body. They are covering his face. And the good news is, they will only grow more painful." The man began to tremble, almost breaking out into a full belly laugh, and then caught himself under his master's glaring eye. "He's trying to treat them with medicine, of course. They always do. It never works."

"Good," Abaddon said, stroking his chin. "Very good. I'm pleased with the progress."

He looked up at the building again. He had promising work going on inside. There were heads of state, presidents, and diplomats here for a series of important talks. He was making headway, planting seeds of distrust, dishonesty, greed, and even a few well-placed thoughts of war here and there. Often that was all it took.

But his mind had continued to drift back toward the pesky quarterling.

He stood, took in a deep breath, and drank down the rest of

the coffee, throwing his cup in the trash can. Stuffing his hands in his pockets, he glanced back down at the other man, who had been watching him carefully.

"It's time to begin phase two," he said.

PART II

TESTS

For look, the wicked bend their bows;
they set their arrows against the strings
to shoot from the shadows
at the upright in heart.

Psalm 11:2

SEVEN

WRONG PLACE AT THE WRONG TIME

The floor of the convent's basement was littered with empty coffee cups and tall glasses of fizzy soft drinks with straws. Almost every chair was occupied by a quarterling, but the room was quiet, having taken on the feel of a library. The written portion of the quarterlings' exams was tomorrow, and class had been cancelled that evening so the students could prepare. The nuns had set up a lounge for them in the basement—complete with bookshelves full of the convent's reference books, some books the angels had brought them, comfortable old couches and chairs, tables for studying, and even some old arcade games—including a Ping-Pong table, a mini basketball hoop, and a foosball table.

Jeremiah was sitting at a table across from Bridget and Lania, supposedly studying, but at the moment he was balancing six books on his head. The girls were giggling.

"Better get to work, Jeremiah," Jonah said, passing him with a fresh soda in his hand. Jeremiah ignored his brother.

Jonah had been studying with David, Eliza, and Julia for the last four hours, and he was exhausted. Jesus' miracles, the order of the plagues in Exodus, the twelve tribes of Israel ... everything was getting mixed up in his head. He was hoping the caffeine from his drink would help him concentrate a little harder.

"Nahum was not a minor prophet, David!" Eliza said, taking off her glasses and flopping them down on the table as Jonah sat back down in his chair.

"Yes, he was," said David, as calmly as possible, but Jonah could see that even his normally unflappable friend was getting heated.

"I can't believe you would even suggest that Nahum would be—"

"Guys!" Jonah broke in. "Come on. Maybe you need to take a break."

Eliza sighed. "No, we need to keep at it."

Jonah watched as she buried her head in her notes again, flipping through note cards and mouthing words to herself. He knew she could keep this up for the rest of the night. No one could touch Eliza when it came to good study habits. David and Julia were about to follow her lead, picking their cards back up too.

"No," Jonah replied. "You need to take a little time and get out of here. It will do you some good. Aren't any of you hungry? I'm starving."

Julia and David looked up at each other and squirmed a little in their chairs. No one answered.

"That's what I thought," said Jonah, standing up again. "Come on, let's go outside and grab some dinner. We'll be gone for an hour and then come back and dig in again. Eliza, what do you say?"

"We're supposed to eat in the dining hall," she said without looking up from her notes.

He rolled his eyes. "We're just going to get more stressed if we stay here, and we all need the fresh air."

"Are you sure it's safe, Jonah?" Julia met his gaze with her dark eyes.

"It's just dinner," he chided. "And let's go somewhere besides a burger joint. Then we'll come straight back. Promise. I want to watch the NBA game tonight anyway. The Heat are playing the Knicks for a preseason charity event at Madison Square Garden!" Jonah's favorite player, LeBron James, was in New York City tonight, playing hoops. He nodded to Eliza, who was glaring at him. "In between study sessions, of course."

They finally relented.

"We need to change clothes first," said Julia, standing up with Eliza.

"Change clothes?" Jonah said. But knowing he'd won them over, he relented. "Okay, sure, we'll do that. Meet you in the lobby in fifteen minutes?"

Jonah and David climbed two flights of stairs in seconds, their long legs taking them three at a time. Jonah changed into a clean T-shirt and a pair of jeans. He saw Abigail's scarf sitting on his dresser and, like he sometimes did, grabbed it and stuffed it in his pocket. For some reason, he liked to carry it with him. It made him feel safer, even though Abigail had been taken up to be with Elohim and couldn't help him any longer.

The girls bounded toward them as Jonah was checking his watch for the sixth time.

"Finally ready?" he said. The girls had taken longer than fifteen minutes.

Eliza smirked. "We're girls. Cut us some slack!"

"Well, I'm ready to eat the biggest steak I can find," said Jonah as they walked out into the dark, humid air and onto the street. A delicious scent wafted through the air from somewhere nearby. "I think we should just follow our noses and see what smells so good."

They walked toward the smell of grilled beef and spices and ran into a crowd of people all headed toward a brightly lit area.

"Times Square," Eliza observed, pointing to the yellow neon billboard advertising a Broadway show. "I haven't been down here in a long time. It's pretty much the craziest place on earth."

Jonah grinned. "And one of the most fun."

"Well, you're in a good mood, considering we have the biggest exam of our lives coming up tomorrow," she said. "And considering all of your . . . skin issues."

"Yeah, well," he said, staring down at his arm. "I need to do something to forget about this for a while. Forgetting about the exam for a few minutes would do you some good too, you know."

They walked along, the crowd growing larger by the second.

"This is the craziest place I've ever seen," said David as they passed a building and the street on their left opened up. "Where do all these people come from?"

Jonah couldn't help but be in awe of the scene too, as more lit street signs and people than he had ever seen in one place came into view.

"It doesn't matter how many times I come here," he said, loudly so they could hear him above the street noise, which was almost as distracting as the lights. "I never get used to this place."

The street was awash with sights and sounds. People were

talking, music was coming out of different restaurants and bars, a guy with an electric guitar was playing on the street corner, and there were booths selling purses, art, and souvenirs lining the sidewalk.

Even though he was excited to be out, Jonah found himself watching people as they walked by, looking for glints of yellow in their eyes. He forced himself to stop. *You can't be paranoid all the time, Jonah.*

"Wonder what's going on there?" Jonah said, pointing to a crowd gathered in front of a wide doorway.

A man outside with a microphone fitted around his ear was working the crowd. He was bald, with golden hoops through each ear, and was holding a hammer and nail up to his face.

Jonah looked up and spotted a sign that read RIPLEY'S BELIEVE IT OR NOT!

"Step forward, step forward," he said, calling out to them and motioning them over. "You don't want to miss what's about to happen. You'll see much more inside, of course, but just so you get a taste of what's to come if you join our show . . ."

He inserted the point of the nail into his nose and, to their shock, began to hammer it in.

"Ewww!" Eliza and Julia said together.

"Awesome!" said Jonah and David.

The five-inch-long nail went all the way in, with no screams from the man. Then, with great drama, he took the back of the hammer and pulled it out again.

"Whew!" he said, rubbing his forehead with his hand. "That wasn't so bad. I was able to miss my brain again."

The crowd went wild.

"Come on," said Eliza, pulling them along. "Let's get out of here before I get sick to my stomach and don't feel like eating anymore."

They walked one more block over, and the street grew much quieter. On the corner, a Mexican restaurant was serving people at tables outside. The smells of something on the grill were much stronger now, and they followed their noses in.

Soon, they were sitting at a table outside, poring over the menu while munching on warm, salty chips and freshly made salsa.

"The steak tacos or the chicken quesadilla," said Eliza. "I just can't decide . . ."

Jonah studied the menu as the waitress came up and asked for their drink orders. "I think I'll have one of these," he said, pointing to a picture of a tall, neon-red-colored drink. "A Lemonade Exploder . . . are they good?"

The waitress looked up from her writing pad. "Yeah. If you think a boatload of sugar and caffeine is a good idea."

"Sounds like a good drink to prepare for an all-night study fest," he said. "I'll take one."

Eliza narrowed her eyes. "You know half of it is lemonade and half is Energy Blitz, right? Which is like three times the caffeine of a normal soft drink?"

But David raised his finger. "I'll have one of those too."

An hour later, after demolishing platefuls of steak tacos, cheesy nachos, and chicken burritos, along with three Lemonade Exploders each for Jonah and David, they settled up their bill and hit the street again.

Jonah was feeling giddy, no doubt from the caffeine and sugar surging through his veins. He and David had begun to play a roughhouse game of leapfrog on the sidewalk, to Julia's amusement and Eliza's frustration.

"Hey, watch this, everybody!" Jonah said as he ran toward the side of a brick building. He pushed his foot up, then another, and for a brief second appeared to scale the wall, before flipping backward and landing on the street.

"Nice move, kid," an older man said as they passed by.

A kid holding his mother's hand pointed at him. "Did you see that, Mommy?"

"Jonah!" Eliza shouted, moving over and grabbing his arm. "You need to calm down! That sugar has gone to your head."

But Jonah wasn't in the mood to listen. As they continued down the street, he had another idea. He hit David in the arm.

"Check this out," he said, and stood in the shadows for a second. Suddenly, he disappeared.

"Jonah!" Eliza called out.

But Jonah wasn't listening.

EIGHT

BELIEVE IT OR NOT

Jonah strolled through the hidden realm, heading toward the crowd. The barker for the Ripley's Believe It or Not! museum was still there, doing his routine. Jonah glanced around to make sure he didn't see any fallen angels, and then behind him to make sure the others could see him.

He moved behind the bald man with the huge nail in his hands, who was about to drive it into his nose again. Summoning his angelic strength, he leaned down and began to lift the box the man was on, just as he hammered the nail in.

"He's floating!" a teenager shouted, pointing at the man's feet. The crowd stepped backward as one, and as the box lifted inches, then a foot, then two feet off the ground, they began to grow hysterical.

Jonah was straining at the weight of the man and the box, but was grinning at Julia and David as he prepared to try to lift him all the way over his head.

"Put him down right now, Jonah Stone!" Eliza said above the noise of the crowd. "Or I promise you, I'll . . . I'll . . . I'll tell Mom and Dad!"

Jonah snickered. "Oh no, Eliza, not that. Please, anything but that."

"Maybe she's right, Jonah," David said, glancing around at the crowd. "These people aren't ready for this, and this guy is really freaking out."

The Ripley's man was moaning softly and waving his arms frantically to keep his balance on the box.

"Okay, okay," Jonah said, finally lowering the box. "I was just trying to have a little fun. You guys don't need to be such—"

But just as he was about to join them, a black, crusty set of hands shot out of the door and yanked him inside the museum. He dropped the box, and the man, onto the hard concrete.

Fingers tightened around Jonah's neck, jerking him backward and throwing him down onto the floor. He slid across the cold tile. Before he could look up, he felt a blow to his stomach, which sent him hurtling into something against the wall. He looked up just as a giant man fell downward with outstretched arms, right on top of him.

"Aaaahhh!"

He grabbed the man's head and was going to push it away when it snapped off from the rest of the body. He was suddenly holding a head in his hands.

"What?" Out of instinct, he threw it across the room and backed himself up against the wall, breathing heavily. He didn't want to look, but he forced himself to glance down at the body as the head rolled across the floor. Expecting blood, he was surprised to see a white, cakey substance inside the neck.

"It's fake, Jonah," he told himself. "I'm in the museum. It's a fake."

The body wasn't the biggest of his concerns, though. He pushed himself up along the wall, hoping his eyes would adjust quickly to the darkened room. There were small groups of people milling around, looking at different displays. They were all gawking at the sight of the tall, headless figure that had fallen. A few had screamed.

Jonah knew they couldn't see him, though. He was searching the room for someone else—the fallen angel who had pulled him in.

The problem was, there were wax figures everywhere, and they looked like real people. Jonah felt his heartbeat race as he looked carefully along the walls. Marilyn Monroe, Justin Bieber, and Taylor Swift were there, unmoving. But where was the fallen one?

The door burst open again, and Eliza, David, and Julia barreled in.

"Jonah!" Eliza called out into the room. She squinted. "Are you in here?"

That was when Jonah happened to look upward. The fallen angel had been sitting motionless, perched on top of a Greek column. But now he screeched loudly and jumped.

They didn't even have time to react before the creature was on top of them. David, Eliza, and Julia crashed to the floor, sprawling under the weight of the dark angel.

"Hey, get off them!" Jonah shouted, hurtling himself across the room. He slammed into the fallen angel, and they both fell into a couple of other statues, sending them into the wall. Bieber's head bounced oddly across the floor, like a misshaped basketball.

The museum visitors panicked. People were screaming and running everywhere, trying to get away from the falling exhibits.

Security guards rushed into the room, but they couldn't see the quarterlings and the Fallen, all now in the hidden realm.

A light flashed right in front of Jonah's eyes, and suddenly he was holding black dust. David stood over him, his bow in hand.

"Thanks," Jonah muttered, pulling himself off the ground.

"You're unbelievable," said Eliza.

Julia folded her arms, raising an eyebrow at him. "I couldn't agree more."

"Guys," Jonah said, holding up his hands. "I know that was—"

The door burst open, cutting him off, and a group of yellow-eyed beasts stood there, searching the room until their eyes landed on them.

The quarterlings began to back away, but more creatures were bounding down the red-carpeted staircase. Jonah didn't bother to count—it was definitely clear that they were outnumbered. They'd been ambushed.

"In here! Quick!" Jonah hissed to his friends, pointing to another set of double doors. It was their only choice, unless they wanted to fight all of the Fallen right there.

They pressed the doors open and entered another museum viewing area. It was a longer, narrower hall than the first one. There was a tall giraffe, standing perfectly still along the wall. Beside it, a group of exotic animals were stuck in different poses, including a giant gorilla, mouth open and arms outstretched.

"Creepy," Eliza whispered.

"Not creepier than Justin Bieber's head," responded Julia.

At the back of the room, a red exit sign hung on the wall.

"That's our way out." Jonah pointed. He glanced back at the double doors, expecting the fallen angels to burst through any second now.

They jogged across the room toward the exit. Jonah hoped it led to a back alley somewhere, and they could make it home from there.

At the back of the room, standing on two giant pedestals, were two creatures that drew Jonah's eyes away from the exit door. They had the heads of lions, with their mouths open wide, showing off their razor-sharp teeth. Their bodies looked as if they belonged to horses, and they had scaly tails like an alligator or crocodile. But the worst part was that the end of each tail sported the head of a snake with long, sharp fangs.

Julia noticed them too and shuddered. "I'm glad those aren't real," she said.

"Yeah, can you imagine?" Jonah said, and headed toward the door again.

But movement from the corner of his eye stopped him short. Jonah turned and watched in horror as the head of one of the creatures slowly pivoted toward them, its eyes turning from dull black to yellow. A roar split the air on his other side, and he knew that the second creature was alive as well.

"Try . . . try to remain calm, everybody," David said. But his voice trembled, anything but calm.

"This is not good at all," Jonah said, reaching for his sword.

His hands grew instantly sweaty, but he pulled the blade and held it up. The strange animals leaped down from the pedestals, hitting the floor with heavy thuds. Their tails swung around, the snake heads hissing.

"They're going to strike!" Eliza cried. She threw her hands up to form a shield.

The lion heads opened their mouths again too. Instead of a roar, though, ash and smoke billowed out, floating across the room. Jonah tried to cover his mouth and nose with his T-shirt. The others were trying to do the same thing. But the fumes seared the inside of his nose anyway, and it felt as though his whole face were on fire. His head spun as the room got darker and darker. *Oh no!* he thought dizzily. *I've killed us all.*

Then everything went completely black.

NINE

ABIGAIL'S SCARF

W here in the world did those statues go?"

Jonah heard the words faintly. Why was he lying on the ground? Cracking one eye open, then slowly the other, he tried to remember where he was. He felt completely disoriented. Two security guards stood in front of him, staring at two large empty pedestals, wondering out loud who possibly could have stolen the wax figures that had been there earlier.

Jonah reached up and rubbed his hand on his face, feeling the pimples all over it. Then the memories from the day came crashing in, one after another. The constant sores, the endless study sessions. Dinner . . .

Images of the barker with the nail in his nose, the fallen angels, and then the awful lion creatures flooded back, and he sat up quickly.

Was any of that real, or was it just a dream? Maybe another one of the visions I've been having . . .

Jonah's question was answered when he saw Eliza lying face-down beside him.

"Eliza! Hey, Eliza!" He crawled over to her, shaking her shoulder. "Come on, wake up!"

"Jonah?" she said drowsily, as if she were talking in her sleep. "My head . . . hurts so much . . ."

He gently rolled her over, facing him.

"Oh, Eliza . . ."

The area around her right eye looked charred, blackened as if it had been hit by the fiery blast. Her eyelid was crumpled and shut. Her left eye opened, looking up at Jonah.

"I . . . I can't open my . . ." She struggled to put words together, clearly still in a daze.

"Shh, Eliza," Jonah said. "It's okay. It's going to be . . . okay."

"What's wrong with my eye?" she finally said.

Jonah swallowed and studied it closely. It was blackened and raw. "It looks like you were hit by the blast from those creatures." Her glasses were lying beside her on the ground, the right lens shattered, the frames twisted like a pretzel.

Slowly, she pushed herself up on her elbows. "David and Julia?"

When Jonah saw them, his heart dropped to the bottom of his sneakers.

They were both sprawled against the wall, a few feet away from each other, unconscious.

"Julia! David!" Jonah rushed over, trying to get a closer look at them. They made no sound or movement, even when he slapped David on the cheek and squeezed Julia's hand hard.

"Come on, guys, wake up!" He was getting frantic now, shaking them harder. "You have to wake up!"

He looked back at Eliza, but she was still in a daze. She would be of no help right now.

There was a burned, jagged hole in David's jeans. Julia had the same kind of thing on her arm, burned through her shirt.

He gently pulled back the cloth of David's jean leg, just to see inside. It wasn't bleeding, but it looked awful. And the smell almost made him lose his dinner.

Jonah slapped them both on the cheeks gently. "Come on, guys," he said, urgency in his voice. "Wake up . . . wake up!"

He was growing more frantic by the second. They weren't responding. He forced the unthinkable out of his mind. *I need to find something to put on their wounds. Maybe they're just in shock.*

He looked around the room, as if somehow he would find a medical kit along the wall. He saw nothing.

Then he remembered. Shoving his hand in his back pocket, he pulled out the brightly colored scarf that had belonged to the prophet Abigail. Without hesitating, he ripped it into three pieces.

He took one and began to tie it around Julia's arm. He did the same with David's leg. The third he tied around Eliza's head, covering her wounded eye. It was all he could think of to do.

They can't be dead, Jonah thought to himself. *They just can't.*

"We have to get you out of here," he said, frowning. "Back to Camilla and the angels. They'll know what to do."

But as he said those words, the pieces of scarf wrapped around their wounds began to subtly change colors. Back and forth, from green to red, yellow, and blue, and back again. At the same time, David's and Julia's eyes began to flutter. Eliza reached up and felt her eye, aware that something was happening.

He looked back and forth, from Abigail's scarf to David's and Julia's faces again. He wasn't sure whether to take the scarves off. What if they were making everything worse?

"Come on." He leaned over them, even more intently. "Come on, wake up, guys!"

Julia opened her eyes suddenly and looked for a split second as if she could still see the lion creature in front of her. She breathed in sharply. But then she sighed and relaxed.

"That was so weird . . . I feel like I just had the worst dream ever . . . ," she said, lifting her arm up to rub her eyes. She saw the scarf. "What is this?"

She quickly pulled it off her arm. The hole in her shirt was still there, but the size of the wound had been drastically reduced. The horrible burn was scabbed over already.

"Ow!" Julia said, lightly touching it. "That stings!"

Jonah was about to tell her she should have seen it a few seconds ago, but David had now opened his eyes too and was examining his leg, pulling it toward him, flexing his knee, and wincing in pain each time.

"That hurts!" he said. But as Jonah inspected the wound again, he saw a mark similar to Julia's, a scab instead of the charred, bloody hole.

He quickly turned to Eliza, who was holding the disintegrating pieces of Abigail's scarf in her hand. Her right eye was still swollen, but not nearly as black as it had been. She could open it, but just barely.

She blinked rapidly for several seconds, then rubbed her eye gently with the palm of her hand. "I still can't see out of this eye," she said. "But it seems better than it was."

That's an understatement, Jonah thought.

He picked up the remaining pieces of Abigail's scarf off the ground. But soon he was holding nothing but a handful of dust.

"Somehow, that scarf is helping us," said Eliza as she stood up and moved toward David and Julia. "Look at their wounds. It's like they've been healing for weeks already. Why would it do that?"

David's eyes looked clearer now, and he tried to stand on his leg. He cried out in pain but continued to pull himself up. It was tender, but he was able to take a few shaky steps.

"I don't know," said David, shaking his head as he studied his leg. "It feels better than it did when it happened but still hurts very badly. All I remember was a flash of light, then the most awful pain I've ever felt. That was right before I blacked out."

"Well, we know the story of Elijah, and how he was taken up in the sky by a chariot of fire, a lot like Abigail," suggested Eliza, still massaging her eye, trying to get it to open wider. "I just never connected the dots on the rest. He dropped his cloak, and remember who picked it up?"

"Elisha," said David. "Hmmm."

"You guys want to explain what you're talking about? Or am I just supposed to guess?" Jonah asked.

"Elisha then was able to use Elijah's cloak to perform a miracle," Julia said, rubbing her arm. "There was power in it. My wound is better too, although I still can't move my arm."

Jonah reached up gently to touch her elbow, but she pulled back, holding her arm with her other hand against her body. She was looking over at the empty pedestals.

"Those creatures . . . ," Julia finally said. "My father used to read us stories out of the book of Revelation. They were creepy. I remember one about the horsemen coming to overrun the earth. But their horses . . ."

"They had the head of a lion and snakes for tails," Eliza said, finishing her sentence.

They stood in the room and caught their breath for a minute.

Jonah thought through all of that and bowed his head in a quiet prayer of thanks. Without Elohim's protection and the scarf, they would be in seriously bad shape. That thought sent a shiver of cold dread up his spine.

But a larger question niggled at his brain, lingering. *Why did they just leave? They had us where they wanted us. And why didn't they hurt me?*

"Looks like you made it through all right, Jonah," Eliza said, without a hint of a smile on her face. David and Julia turned toward him too, studying him up and down.

"Yeah," said Julia. "How did *you* end up being the only one unharmed?"

"Guys, I don't know," Jonah started. "I didn't mean to get you hurt."

"They're right, you know," David said. "We could have easily been killed. What were you thinking, out there on the sidewalk?"

Jonah opened his mouth but shut it again. He didn't have an answer.

Eliza sighed loudly, looking at her bent glasses. "Let's just get out of here."

They walked slowly out of the museum. Eliza could see from only one eye, and Julia's arm wasn't moving. David's leg was a mess. He reluctantly let Jonah support him on his shoulder as he limped along.

Jonah wished he could take all of their injuries on himself. But they were right. It was his fault they'd caught the attention of the Fallen, and for some crazy reason, he was the only one who made it out without a scratch.

TEN

An Unforeseen
Opportunity

A horse pulled the carriage along the cold, empty street beside
Central Park, the wheels grating along the asphalt. The only
other sound was that of the wind whipping through the trees,
bringing a knife of cold air into the streets. There were no other
carriages out tonight. The others had finished giving scenic rides
to their last customers hours ago, deemed it too cold for more pas-
sengers, and gone home.

The fallen angel waited on the corner as he had been told,
watching the carriage move toward him. He didn't know what to
expect, only that he had been summoned in a hurry to the street
corner, where he should await further orders.

The carriage rolled to a stop beside him, driven by a tall, thin
man in a black driver's coat and top hat, holding the reins loosely
and looking straight ahead, his face covered by shadow.

"Get in."

The voice came from the passenger seat of the carriage. The fallen angel stepped up two small steps in and sat beside a man in a suit and tie. The man leaned forward enough that the streetlamp caught the side of his face as his eyes fixed on the new passenger.

The fallen angel's mouth dropped open. He had been told only where to meet. He hadn't been notified that he would be speaking with Abaddon himself.

"My lord!" he said, bowing his head as his hands began to tremble. "I . . . I didn't know it would be you . . ."

"Just sit down, shut up, and listen carefully," Abaddon said, turning now to look out at the trees. The driver took them down a pathway in the park. "We've had an opportunity fall into our laps this evening, thanks to our quarterling friends. Specifically, their golden boy, Jonah Stone himself."

The fallen one nodded. He wanted to tell the Evil One that he had already received a report of the incident in Times Square, but he was afraid to open his mouth again.

"It seems that he let his pride get the best of him," Abaddon said, smiling for the first time. He began to chuckle, which made even the fallen angel smile nervously. "Nothing like a little old-fashioned sin to get you into trouble. It's time to take advantage of his mistakes and make him pay. His friends are not too happy with him right now. Nor should they be . . . he almost got them killed."

They drove past a couple of overstuffed trash cans reeking of garbage yet to be emptied. He breathed in deeply, enjoying the smell, and continued.

"I want you and your crew to do whatever you can to turn his friends and his family against him. Use this incident to make sure they are very angry with him. And make sure he knows he is totally, utterly alone. I want him to think that not even Elohim Himself can help him get his friends back."

The fallen angel nodded, working up the courage to finally talk. "If I may, my lord, what of Jonah himself? A well-placed arrow by one of my most talented men would certainly do—"

Abaddon turned quickly, his face growing bony and grotesque, eyes blazing red, just inches from the underling's face. "I told you what I want you to do! Do not, under any circumstances, deviate from my orders. Is that clear?"

The fallen angel cringed, pushing himself back against the side of the carriage and looking down at his hands. "Yes, my master. Forgive me."

"Don't worry about the boy," Abaddon said, backing off, but clearly still annoyed. "I have someone specifically assigned to him and his family."

As he said those words, the driver turned to face them, grinning wickedly, his face suddenly morphing from a bearded human to only a greenish mist and fierce eyes.

The fallen angel drew in a sharp breath, seeing for the first time who it was. The driver slapped the reins down, and the horse stopped.

"Yes, sir! Consider it done, my master," the fallen angel uttered, scrambling to get out of the carriage as fast as possible.

"Very well, then," Abaddon called out. "I hope that's the case. For your sake."

He watched the carriage continue down the dark street and heard the laughter of two voices trail away through Central Park.

ELEVEN

Exams Begin

The walk home was as quiet as it was slow. Eliza, David, and Julia were angry, and Jonah didn't blame them. He knew better than to try to talk to them right now. They needed time to cool off. The priority now was getting them back to Camilla and the nuns, who hopefully could help them with their injuries.

He was mad at himself too. Why had he decided to show off? He knew better than that. He'd almost gotten all of them killed.

Camilla took one look at the three wounded quarterlings and ushered them into one of the small offices in the convent, where there were a couple of chairs and a cot. Marcus and Taryn emerged from the back door and into the hallway.

"Get Samuel!" Camilla barked at Marcus. "And Bashir and Sister Patricia! Now!"

She studied their wounds, then turned to Jonah with a cold gaze. "In a few minutes, you're going to tell me everything, but right now, you'd better start praying."

He did as he was told, closing his eyes and offering prayers to Elohim for his friends. As his heart quieted and another wave of reality hit him, he had to blink back tears, especially as he prayed for Eliza's vision to return.

Soon, Pastor Bashir and Sister Patricia joined him in prayer, the tendrils of light from their prayers joining together in the hidden realm, pouring upward through the ceiling. Samuel was carefully studying their wounds, grave concern on his face.

"No doubt this is the work of the Steeds of the Horsemen," he said, standing up. "No human medicine will help. Their healing is in Elohim's hands."

Camilla and Samuel joined the rest in prayer. After what felt like more than an hour, Camilla said, "Amen," and summoned the Angel School instructors into her office. Jonah walked out into the hallway behind them. He knew he shouldn't be eavesdropping, but he couldn't help himself.

"I'm concerned that we are putting these kids in harm's way by even having them here." The distinct voice of Pastor Bashir rose above the others. "You all know that I am all about faith and risk, when necessary. But we need to make sure we are wise as well."

Another voice spoke, but it was softer, and Jonah couldn't tell what was being said.

"The animals certainly fit the description of those described in Revelation," came Samuel's higher-pitched tone. "They were certainly Steeds of the Horsemen, no doubt about it."

"Which means," a strong voice interrupted—Jonah thought it was probably Marcus—"that we need to go after them now, before they do any more damage! If Abaddon is using those creatures to do his bidding, there's no telling what else he's planning to do with them."

"They were being foolish." Taryn's voice rose. "Jonah was showing off. If they hadn't gone out, none of this would have happened."

"She's right," the weary voice of Camilla finally said. "They took a risk and almost paid a high price for it. They were in the wrong place at the wrong time. I will discuss this with them. Marcus, there is no need to go on a wild-goose chase. I'm sure Abaddon has the creatures far away by now. If he has something planned, he won't want to risk us putting a stop to it. It was a blessing that Jonah had Abigail's scarf, no doubt. In the meantime, no students are to leave the convent. Is that clear?"

There were murmurs of approval, and Jonah quickly backed away from the door.

The angels emerged, along with Pastor Bashir. Marcus glared at Jonah but passed by without a word, like the rest.

"Jonah!" Camilla's voice called. "A word, if you please."

After ten minutes of being reprimanded by the angel in her office, he wanted to run for the door. She threatened to call his parents, scolded him about putting the entire school in danger, and informed him that because of the incident, no one would be allowed to leave school property without heavy supervision from the angels.

She dismissed him with a flick of her wrist. "That will be all."

That was fine with Jonah. He found David, Julia, and Eliza ambling down the hallway toward the stairs.

"Thanks a lot, Jonah," Eliza said. Since it was Eliza, Jonah wasn't sure if she was more upset at the lack of vision in her eye or that he'd gotten them in big trouble with all of their instructors. She had never made a teacher mad at her in her entire life.

"I'm sorry," he said slowly, in almost a whisper.

She turned back toward him, her features softening. Her mouth hung open for a few seconds as if she was thinking about saying something.

Just then, Jonah heard a faint sound, almost a whisper, but not quite. He turned to Eliza's left, where it seemed to come from, but saw nothing. Suddenly, Eliza's mouth snapped shut, and she turned her back on Jonah again, continuing down the hall with Julia.

Jonah stood in the hall for a few seconds, blinking. His gut told him something wasn't right. Quickly, he prayed, entering the hidden realm.

A flash of darkness shot out of the corner of his eye. Before he could see what it was—if it was anything—it was gone. Jonah ran down to the corner but only found an empty hallway.

Jonah leaned his head on the wall, pressing his hands against it as he prayed again. He reentered the visible realm and watched as David followed Eliza and Julia, limping down the hall.

"David," Jonah called out. "I'm sorry, okay? I didn't know what was going to happen."

David rubbed his leg and didn't look back. "I'm sure you didn't, Jonah. But still . . ."

Jonah heard him clunk his way up the first flight of steps. Leaning back against the wall, he pressed his fingers against his temples for a few seconds. He was exhausted but didn't feel like going to his room yet to face David. He wandered downstairs, made himself a cup of tea, and flung himself into an easy chair.

Rupert, Ruth, and Carlo were studying quietly at a table in the corner and barely looked up at Jonah. The written portion of their exams was set for nine o'clock in the morning. And thanks to him, his friends were in no shape to study. They were going to be even angrier with him when they realized that. The feeling of being unprepared only made him sink lower into the chair. *I'll study*, he told himself. But his head was throbbing again. *I just need to close my eyes for a few seconds.*

When he opened his eyes, the other quarterlings were gone and sunlight was streaming through the few small windows near the ceiling. He groaned and closed his eyes again. If it wasn't for midterms today . . .

Midterms.

Jonah sat up and looked at the clock on the wall. It couldn't be. The clock read 8:56 a.m.

"No, no, no!" he said, jumping up and running for the door.

Frantically, he tried to remember everything he had studied the day before as he ran down the hallway. But his brain seemed to be moving in a hundred directions at once, and yet not heading anywhere. And his head was hurting. With each step he took, the pounding grew worse.

He ran into the boys' bathroom and splashed some water on his face.

"Ow!"

The water stung the boils, which had multiplied once again. With his hair sticking out in every direction, his eyes half-open, and the red splotches on his face and body, he shook his head in disgust.

But there was no time to do anything about it now.

He burst into the classroom across the hall just as Samuel was passing out the test to the quarterlings, all sitting at desks. Every head in the silent room whipped around to see who it was. Eliza looked him over for a few seconds, scowled, and turned back toward Samuel.

Frederick raised his eyebrows. "Dude, you look like—"

"I said complete silence is required for this test," Samuel interrupted, glaring at him. "Now remember, class, there are different tests for the different age groups. The midterms are specifically designed for you."

Jonah slumped into a chair in the back, shielding his face from everyone for a minute as he tried to gather his thoughts. Samuel placed a thick stack of parchment paper in front of him. The cover page said:

Midterm Examination
Jonah Stone, Quarterling

In spite of the fancy lettering and paper, it didn't look that different from tests he had taken in school. He breathed in deeply, picked up the pencil on the desk, and began.

Four hours later, mentally and physically exhausted, he set his pencil down. The only student who hadn't finished yet was Eliza. Jonah figured she was probably going over it for the third or fourth time, just to make sure she got every answer right.

Jonah, on the other hand, wasn't sure he'd gotten anything correct. His head hurt, and as he stood up, he felt light-headed. He grabbed onto the back of the chair to steady himself.

"Jonah, are you okay?" Samuel asked, stepping forward to take his test. "You look a little pale."

"I think so," he said, trying to appear tough. But then he added, "I don't know . . . my head is hurting. It's probably just all the stress and excitement."

Samuel studied him carefully. "Perhaps. I imagine it would do you a great deal of good to get some fresh air."

"Yeah," he mumbled as he headed for the door. "You're probably right."

Jonah sighed loudly as he walked down the hallway alone. He felt as if he had struggled with every part of the test. Even the stuff he knew that he knew—like the order of the books of the Bible, the names of the twelve disciples, and the Egyptian plagues—didn't come to him like it normally did.

He trudged up the stairs, hoping he could get some sleep.

"Jonah," came a voice from above him in the stairwell.

He spun his head upward, jumping a little more than he normally would have.

"Sorry to startle you," the voice said. Nathaniel, the lieutenant colonel of the Second Battalion of the Angelic Forces of the West, stood above him on the steps, wearing his glittering silver armor.

"Nathaniel," Jonah said. "I was . . . I was just heading to my room to get some sleep. I had a long night. And then the midterms and everything . . ."

"Your presence is requested," he said, ignoring Jonah's comment and glancing upward. "Upstairs."

TWELVE

Rooftop Encounter

Jonah blinked. "Oh, okay. Do you need to talk to me about something?"

"Not me," he said. "My orders are to retrieve you and escort you to the roof. Someone is waiting to speak with you there. That's all I can tell you. Now, if you will . . ."

He motioned for Jonah to follow him.

Jonah's curiosity suddenly grew stronger than his desire to take some aspirin and get a nap. They arrived at the top level of the convent, and for the first time, he noticed a metal ladder on the wall in the stairwell. It led up toward a rusted trapdoor with a handle. Nathaniel grabbed the rung of the ladder, pulled himself upward until his feet could grab the bottom rung, and began to climb.

"I guess this is how we get to the roof," Jonah said softly. Soon he was pushing his way through the trapdoor. He wondered who needed to see him on the roof.

The hinged steel door slammed down on the asphalt roof

with a clang so loud that it made Jonah freeze. He looked around but couldn't see anything except an air-conditioning unit right beside him and a short wall on the other side. Jonah stepped up onto the rooftop.

"This way," Nathaniel's gruff voice called out to him.

Jonah walked forward, looking all around. Even though the building was low, he was able to see several large skyscrapers towering in the not-too-far distance. He figured they were part of Rockefeller Center, which was several blocks north.

Warrior angels lined the side of the roof that looked down over the street and the back of the building as well, which led to the alleyway. Some were focused downward in their watch, while others, upward, into the sky. Marcus had said they watched day and night, never tiring, vigilant in their protection of those they had been assigned to.

Jonah was glad of it, especially since guardian angels were assigned to their parents and the rest of the quarterlings' families.

Nathaniel walked over to the wall and took his place beside the other angels. Jonah was about to follow him and ask him what he was supposed to do now when a flash of light suddenly stopped him. It felt like the flash of a camera behind him. *Is someone taking pictures?* Jonah spun around to see a massive angel with wings so large it seemed they could spread across the entire roof if opened wide. His armor was silver and gold and scarred in different places, as if it had seen its share of battles.

"Archangel Michael," Jonah said, somehow simultaneously surprised and a little afraid. They had met before, briefly, in the woods behind Jonah's home in Peacefield, at the end of Jonah and Eliza's epic journey to rescue their kidnapped mother. Jonah gave a quick, unsure bow. The angel watched Jonah and returned his greeting.

"Well, Jonah," Michael said, walking over to get a closer look at him. "I heard about your . . . condition." He grabbed Jonah's arm from his side and held it up, inspecting it. "But it looks even worse in person. How does it feel?"

"Not too bad, sir." Jonah wasn't sure how to take his comment and found himself staring down at his feet.

Michael nodded but frowned, watching the boy intently with a look on his face Jonah couldn't decipher. It was a knowing gaze from sharp eyes Jonah could be swallowed up into if he stared too long.

"I heard about the attack last night too," Michael said, his eyes inviting Jonah to explain himself.

"Well, yeah," Jonah said, scratching his head. "I was . . . well . . . I shouldn't have been goofing around, and it got us into some trouble. These creatures, they seemed like they were straight out of the book of Revelation."

"The Steeds of the Horsemen," Michael said. "Very danger-ous beasts. Jonah, you would do well to be a little more cautious."

Jonah nodded miserably. "I know. It's all my fault. I know what I did wrong—and believe me, it won't happen again. But what I can't figure out is why they didn't finish the job. Why we're all still alive. And I didn't get hurt at all . . ."

The archangel grunted but offered no answer. "Some ques-tions can only be explained by Elohim Himself."

Jonah could tell Michael couldn't—or wouldn't—shed any light on his question. He deflated on the inside, like air leaking from a basketball. But he'd felt the same way with Camilla in the past too. Sometimes the angels were just unwilling to give him the information he felt he needed.

When he was about to turn and say good night, Michael's heavy hand landed on Jonah's shoulder.

"This is not why I summoned you here on the rooftop, Jonah. I wanted to show you something," he said, his eyes still knowing yet mysterious. He pulled Jonah along with him to the corner of the roof, two warrior angels moving silently out of their way. "You're a prophet. You have abilities that you have only begun to realize. You can see things that most of the others like yourself are not allowed to see. Some things not even angels can see. It is a privilege."

"It's a burden," Jonah snapped back, surprising even himself.

Michael nodded. "It is both."

Even though they were standing in the sunlight, Jonah shivered. He knew he should feel nothing but honored that Elohim had chosen him for such a huge responsibility, but he couldn't help it—he didn't like being singled out. And he was nervous about letting Elohim down.

Michael stood on the edge of the building with him. "You must remember that you don't get to choose the path you walk down, Jonah," he said, looking up at the hazy sky. "Only how you walk down it. Are you ready?"

"Ready for what?"

Michael pushed his arm across the air in front of them slowly.

The sky disappeared, and suddenly the whole scene transformed, not only in front of him, but all around him too. He was alone. Michael was no longer there, nor were the sentinel angels. Glancing down, he realized his shoes were gone, and his feet were, in fact, touching sand! All around him, he heard the unmistakable sound of waves caressing a shoreline.

Jonah took in the scene around him with his mouth open. He was on a sandy beach, and the sun was beating down, warming his skin. A breeze blew, and beautiful crystal blue waves crashed against the shore, lapping backward, only to be overtaken by another wave, then another.

A grove of palm trees sprang up from the sandy soil to his left. To his right was the widest, flattest beach he had ever seen.

Something compelled him to walk, and he began to make a slow path beside the water, his feet making deep footprints in the soft sand, his senses attuned to the saltiness in the air and the breeze rustling through his hair.

He felt a presence behind him, and suddenly he knew he wasn't alone. Someone was there. Turning his head, he watched as a man in a wetsuit came running up, both hands holding a surfboard on his head.

"Jonah, wait up!" the man called out.

How does he know my name?

But he waited for the man to catch up with him. He had a shaggy beard that reminded him of his father's, but longer. His hair, which was barely tamed, hung down to his shoulders. He was wet, like he had just come out of the water. He pushed the tangled strands out of his face, smiling easily.

"Where is this place?" asked Jonah. "Who are you? And how do you know who I am?"

The man held his hand out to the ocean. "We're at the beach, of course," he said, winking at Jonah. "I've been surfing these waves all day. Beautiful, isn't it?"

Jonah stared at him for a few seconds, feeling confused, realizing that the man didn't answer his other two questions. Finally, though, Jonah nodded, watching the waves crash on the shore again. "Yeah, it is beautiful," he admitted. "The most beautiful beach I've ever seen." *I just don't know if it's real.*

"Oh, it's real, all right," the man said. Jonah did a double take, wondering if he'd actually said it out loud. "Elohim has created some incredible places in this world of His."

"Did you just . . . ?" Jonah didn't complete his sentence.

"Hear what you were thinking?" The man laughed.

Jonah wasn't sure how he felt about that. "That's kind of weird."

"I know." He laughed. "Don't worry. I won't hold any of it against you. Listen, Jonah, I understand how you must be feeling. But I assure you, the visions you have are just as real as anything else."

"So that's what this is," Jonah said. "Just another vision?"

As they walked along, the man picked up a sand dollar and studied it as if it were the most interesting thing he had ever seen. He then tossed it into the water as he spoke.

"You do have a gift, Jonah, to be sure," the man said, ignoring the question. "Elohim made you very unique and special. Pretty cool, I think."

"If you say so," Jonah muttered.

The man stopped, turned toward Jonah, and looked at him with deep concern etched on his face. "I know so, my friend. It's time you start believing that too."

He grabbed his board with both hands and pointed it toward the waves.

"They look good out there, don't they? Nothing like riding a great wave," he said, looking long over the horizon. He turned his attention back to Jonah again. "A lot of things are going to happen—a lot of good things. And I'm not going to lie to you; some bad things are going to happen too. Some that will make you question everything you believe and everything you live for.

I just want you to remember that, no matter what, on your darkest day, when all hope seems lost, Elohim always walks with you. And nothing is wasted on Him."

Jonah found himself unsettled at those words, but something about the man made him feel relaxed too—more relaxed than he'd felt since he found out he was a quarterling. This man was on his side—he was a friend.

The man reached out and touched Jonah on the arm gently. A surge of electricity shot through him. His entire body jolted, full with energy, and something more: the warm, igniting presence of Elohim. It pulsed through him, moving from his arm into his stomach and out to his fingers and toes. His heart felt at ease, and it was hard to even remember what he was so worried about before. Because right now, all he felt was a deep sense of peace.

He looked back down at his arm again, where the man had touched him, and suddenly he was back on the roof. Michael's hand was there now, instead of the beach surfer's.

"Whoa."

Jonah stood there, trying to catch his breath. He still felt the same peace, just as if he were still on the beach. Now, however, the angels standing watch over the building came into view again. Michael waited quietly beside him, letting him get his bearings.

"How long was I gone?"

Michael tilted his head. "Gone?"

"The man on the beach," Jonah said. "Who was he?"

Jonah realized he hadn't even thought to ask him. All he wanted to do was go back and surf with that guy, despite the fact that he'd never ridden a wave in his life. Now that he was back on top of the building, the peace he had felt began to fade just a little.

"Whatever you saw was between you and Elohim," answered

Michael. "But you can be sure that you saw and heard from Him, and He let you know exactly what He wanted to."

Jonah thought about that. He hadn't received any answers. But he was reassured by the presence of that man. He looked down at his arms and saw the marks still there. His head began to throb again. *He said that good things were going to happen, but some bad things too.*

He wanted to focus only on the hope that good was around the corner. But he found his mind drifting more toward darker things.

THIRTEEN

New Morning,
New Possibilities

The usually quiet Convent of Saint John of the Empty Tomb was buzzing with energy Wednesday morning. Camilla had announced that all the quarterlings should be ready by ten o'clock to begin their practical exams, the skills-testing portion of midterms. She also said their grades from their written exams would be posted outside her office door by nine thirty.

Breakfast was served promptly at eight thirty, and for once, all thirteen of the quarterlings were there on time, chatting about the exams over their food. They hovered over Eliza, David, and Julia, making sure the injured kids had enough to eat and drink. The three were still in a lot of pain, and the other quarterlings shot Jonah dark looks. He knew that everyone blamed him for their injuries. He blamed himself for getting them hurt too.

As Jonah quietly filled his plate with food, he heard a sound again. Like a low whisper behind him. He spun around, half expecting to see a crouching figure in the room, but he saw only the quarterlings busily eating.

He sat alone at the end of the table and was taking a bite of food when he heard it again. He turned to look at the others, searching each of them intently.

"What do you keep looking at?" Hai Ling said, scowling. "Is there something you want to say?"

Jonah looked past her, his eyes darting around the room. There was nothing there.

"I'm not looking at anything," he mumbled, stuffing another bite in his mouth.

He had woken up with another splitting headache, and the quick movements were making him dizzy. He rubbed his forehead with his fingers for a while. Picking up his knife, he scraped the back of his hands, trying to satisfy the itches the boils gave him. He felt more stares as he did this, but he couldn't help it. The itching was almost unbearable.

Camilla had instructed them to gather in the basement room and wait for her arrival. At precisely ten o'clock, with a flash of light, seven messenger angels appeared in front of them.

The angels were all dressed alike, with long robes glittering a silvery light like a sky full of stars. Camilla stood in the middle of them.

She let go of the male angel's arm. "Thank you for the ride, Marcello," she said, nodding to him. "Nothing like traveling on the arm of a messenger angel."

Camilla was wearing a brightly colored robe herself. It seemed to reflect every shade of the rainbow, depending on how she turned.

"Are we going to go on a ride again?" Jeremiah asked, eyeing the messenger angels.

"Yes, indeed!" Camilla confirmed. "You all look ready. And it's time to go. The first part of the skills examination is about to begin."

"I don't suppose you're going to tell us where we're going?" asked Eliza, her curiosity piqued.

Camilla's eyes shone even brighter. "Now why would I want to tell you a thing like that and spoil the surprise?"

The messenger angels said nothing but held out their arms toward the kids. Stepping forward, Jonah touched the arm of one of the angels, who glanced at his face, covered with the red marks. She smiled ever so slightly at him.

Camilla gave them all one last look. "All right, Marcello. Let's get this show on the road."

Except that Jonah didn't hear her say the word *road*. Because the next thing he knew, he saw a flash of light in front of him, felt his feet lift off the ground, and then an uncomfortable squeezing sensation all over his body.

"I'm never going to get used to that," he muttered to himself, bending over to catch his breath, his feet back on the ground.

Looking up, he blinked a couple of times and saw that he and the others were standing in a lush, green field. It was a flat expanse with markings on it, surrounded by trees, with rolling hills of farmland and sheep in the distance. The sun appeared to be setting, casting a warm glow on everything and everyone Jonah could see.

The messenger angels who were with them had disappeared, gone in the blink of an eye.

"Where are we?" he heard Eliza ask.

Camilla was dusting herself off. "Welcome to Ireland!" she exclaimed. "We will travel to other parts of the world for the different tests. I love this place. Isn't it beautiful?"

"Ireland? Awesome!" said Eliza. She breathed in the cool, fresh air and studied the field and the trees in front of her with her good eye. "It is beautiful. I guess that explains why it's so green here."

An angel moved into the clearing in front of them.

"Nathaniel!" Jeremiah shouted, waving to the warrior angel.

Nathaniel nodded at him. "Welcome to the skills portion of your midterm examination," he said. "The first challenge is angelic defense. Since everyone has to acquire skills in defense, whether you have a shield or not, everyone will participate. Eliza, David, and Julia—we don't want to strain your injuries, so you have the option to sit out this part of your exam and be graded later through an oral presentation. Or, if you feel up to it, you may participate now."

Jonah felt the heated glances of the quarterlings, and he kicked at the grass at his feet.

David and Julia both stepped backward. Jonah wasn't surprised. There was no way David could run on his leg. He could barely walk. And Julia wouldn't be able to produce her shield since she was still having trouble moving her arm.

What surprised him was that Eliza stayed put.

"Eliza," Jonah whispered, leaning toward her. "Don't you think you should sit out this time? How are you going to be able to—"

"Don't tell me what I can and cannot do," she snapped at him, looking straight ahead at Nathaniel, who for the first time allowed his lips to curl into a small smile.

He gave her a slight nod. "Very well then. Marcus?"

Marcus flew in from behind and settled in front of them. "As you can see, there is a field in front of you marked by four posts, signifying out of bounds. If you go beyond that boundary, you will be disqualified and receive no points. The goal is to stay untouched for as long as possible."

Ruth, David's sister, raised a shaky hand. "Untouched by what, exactly?"

Marcus's eyes glittered. "Your job is to avoid anything that comes at you. You may not use any weapons—only defensive measures."

"But how is that fair?" Rupert asked. "We can't all make the shield of faith. Won't the ones who can have an advantage over the rest of us?"

Some of the other quarterlings nodded. They had been thinking the same thing.

"But you are all able to defend yourselves, yes?" Camilla said, moving around the students now. "All of you have gifts. Even though, yes, some of you are able to use the shield of faith, there are other ways to defend yourselves from an attack. Think about your gifts, use them, and be as creative as you can."

Jonah pondered this, knowing the angel was right. The butterflies in his stomach didn't go away, though. But another feeling was creeping in too. He saw Frederick eyeing him with that old competitive look. Jonah met it with his own stare.

He wanted to do the best.

They were separated, each going with a different messenger angel to a place just on the outside of the markers lining the field. The quarterlings were to start an equal distance apart, in their own section of the grass.

Nathaniel, Marcus, Camilla, and Taryn floated up over the field so they could have an uninterrupted view of the test.

The announcer dropped his hand just as the sun went behind the trees. Jonah's breathing immediately quickened, and he picked up his head and turned around, trying to see any movement he could. He bent his knees, squinting his eyes into the sudden darkness.

The problem was, he couldn't see anything. He tried to look across the field, and like lightbulbs turning on, he saw some of the quarterlings raise the shield of faith. One, two, three, four. *That should be it,* Jonah thought. To his knowledge, only Eliza, Rupert, Carlo, Bridget, and Julia had the gift. And Julia was sitting out.

He waited, not knowing what to expect. Everything in him wanted to reach down and pull out his angelblade, but this was a defense-only competition. He had been instructed not to use that or his bow.

That left only one option. He prayed quickly while his eyes remained open, surveying the scene.

"Elohim, make my feet fast again, by Your power and strength," he whispered.

He peeked down at his feet, watching his basketball shoes change into leather sandals.

He was as ready as he was going to be.

A scream came from the other side of the field. Jonah wasn't sure but thought it sounded like Bridget. His pulse quickened again.

Suddenly he saw yellow eyes.

A creature emerged from the darkness, running straight for him. *They are letting the Fallen attack us?* Jonah thought frantically.

He turned and ran in the opposite direction, looking back over his shoulder. With his angel speed, his pursuer was having a hard time catching up. But just as he turned his head forward again, he saw another one coming straight at him.

Jonah veered to the right, coming across some of the other quarterlings. As he blurred by, he saw Rupert holding his shield steady. He was under attack from three fallen angels. His shield was growing dimmer. Should he stop and help? But Jonah continued running and saw Eliza's shield, bright and glowing, sparks flying all around. Her shield was being pummeled.

Another fallen angel, then another, had joined the chase for Jonah, and he wasn't sure how long he could keep this up. The field was big, but there still wasn't enough space to outrun them for long.

He passed a few others who had realized they could run too—Frederick, Hai Ling, and Lania. Jonah pushed himself harder. He was moving fast, maybe faster than he had ever run before. He wove in and out of obstacles at such a quick pace that everything around him had become a blur.

As he turned again, though, looking behind him, he slammed into something so hard that he immediately bounced off it and fell backward. For a few seconds, all he saw were bright, hazy splotches of light. He pressed the sides of his head with his hands, trying to stop the sudden throbbing.

Jonah blinked a few times and looked up in time to see yellow eyes glaring over him. He pushed himself back on the grass and reached down for his sword. But before he could pull it out, the face in front of him changed. Yellow eyes changed to blue, and the ugly face to that of a kind, friendly angel. Two more stepped over him. One reached down, extending a hand, which Jonah slowly took. *They weren't real. The Fallen were just angels in disguise.* Jonah breathed a sigh of relief. He wasn't going to be ripped to shreds after all.

"Not too bad, young quarterling," the angel said. "The test is over now."

"You were fast out there," a shorter, stocky one commented. "Almost too fast for us."

Jonah shook his head a few times, trying to get it clear. "Not fast enough to miss that wall, or whatever that was. Oh, man . . ." He leaned over, catching his breath again.

"That wall would be me," a deep voice said. He looked up to see an enormous angel, a head above the others, standing with his arms crossed.

Jonah continued to rub his head. "Oh, well, that makes sense."

Eliza. Jeremiah.

His brother and sister immediately came to his mind. Searching the field, he began to walk toward the other kids and angels he saw.

"Eliza!" he called out. "Jeremiah! Where are you guys?"

He walked past a dazed Rupert but stopped long enough to check on him. He was doing fine, although complaining about something to one of the angels.

"My father's going to hear about this!" he overheard the boy say.

Jonah finally found his brother standing beside a couple of angels, who were laughing at something he was saying.

"How'd it go, Jeremiah?" asked Jonah. "You okay?"

"Yeah, it was actually pretty fun," he said, smiling. "I don't have a shield or sandals like you guys, so I just tried to use my small size to hide behind people. It worked," he said. "For a while anyway. Then this guy came up and tackled me to the ground." He punched an angel in the arm. The angel chuckled again.

"This one, we're going to have to watch out for," the angel said, rubbing Jeremiah's head.

Jonah found Eliza in the far corner of the field, resting on the grass. She was still rubbing her eye, but her look toward Jonah had softened just a little.

"So how'd it go?" he asked, standing back a few steps.

"It was tough, especially with only one eye," she said, "but it was a good test. I was able to hang in there a pretty long time. I didn't expect the angels to be disguised as the Fallen, that's for sure."

"Me neither. To be honest, I thought they were real. I guess I should have known they wouldn't let the Fallen attack us like that. But I'm sure you did great," Jonah said, trying to be encouraging. "You're the best I know at the shield of faith."

She deflected his compliment. "Yeah, but I still got caught," she said, frowning. "I guess we're about to find out how everyone did." She pointed up to Nathaniel and the other angels, still floating above.

His voice boomed across the field, almost as if it were magnified. "Well done, my friends. That was an excellent performance. All of you are to be commended for your bravery! You each will receive points for your performance, with everything taken into account, including the gifts you were able to use and how long you were able to last against our so-called fallen angels."

Taryn handed him a piece of paper, and he studied it for a moment.

"Receiving As on this portion of exams are the following quarterlings," Nathaniel said. As he spoke, the area around Jonah started to glow, separating him from the others around him. Jonah fidgeted, not enjoying the spotlight on him alone. "Jonah! Excellent job avoiding capture for so long and using the sandals of speed to your advantage. Bravo!"

A light smatter of applause came from some of the students. He nodded toward them but couldn't help but notice David and Julia on the sidelines, hands in their pockets.

"Also with an A, we have another member of the Stone family. Eliza!" She brushed a stray curl out of her face and stepped forward, into the light. "Beautiful use of the shield of faith, especially considering your injury," Nathaniel said. "Very well done!"

She blushed as the cheers arose for her, much louder than they had for Jonah.

"There is one more competitor earning an A, who displayed such an amazing display of speed and agility that I daresay even among the angels we don't see such athleticism and skill very often," the angel said, pausing for a few seconds. Jonah saw the spotlight shining across the field on one of the quarterlings. "Let's hear it for Frederick!"

The spotlight shone on him in the other corner of the field. He held both hands up in the air, pumping his fists.

"Okay, okay, Frederick," Nathaniel said, smiling. "These are the top three performers today. And I'm sure you'd like to know in what order they rank. First place goes to . . . Frederick!"

The quarterlings cheered as Jonah felt his heart sink.

"In second, we have Eliza! Which means third place belongs to Jonah."

Jonah walked over to Frederick, wanting to shake his hand, but he was being crowded by most of the other quarterlings, as well as Marcus and Taryn and a few of the messenger angels, offering their own congratulations and encouragement.

He decided to save his handshake for later and walked back under the trees, trying to tell himself that third place was nothing to hang his head about.

FOURTEEN

A SHADOW
IN THE HALLWAY

Pale moonlight shone through the window at the end of the silent hallway as M'chala glided just above the wooden floor. He moved like one part fallen angel, two parts fog and shadow, searching, probing, pausing in front of each door. Then down to another, then another. He passed his gnarled hand along the room numbers, sensing the presence behind each door but moving on.

He came to one, though, and suddenly stopped, tracing his finger along the numbers on the door. Closing his eyes, he held his hand flat in front of it, until it almost rested on the wood.

The boy was in here. There was no doubt.

M'chala slid under the door, flowing from the hallway into the room, a dark and quiet mist of shadow. He stood up again and momentarily lingered over the African boy's sleeping body. He held out his finger over his face for a few seconds, then down toward his stomach, pondering the many diseases he could inflict with but one touch.

He almost did it, just because he could. But this wasn't whom he had come for. Reluctantly, he backed away.

Moving to the other side of the room, he hovered for a while over the snoring shape underneath the sheet. All that was visible was a shock of dark, shaggy hair. M'chala held his hand over the boy's head. The boy groaned and turned over.

The spirit held his index finger out directly over the boy's chest. With relish, he poked it to the edge of his skin, just above his heart, and then farther in.

Jonah twisted and flailed to the other side of the bed but did not wake up. He would only remember it as another bad dream, if he remembered it at all.

When he was done, M'chala pulled his finger back and watched the boy fall into a peaceful sleep once again.

He left the room as quietly as he had arrived. His work was complete. For now.

∿

All Jonah could see was white. He blinked his eyes several times, trying to allow them to adjust. Squinting them, diminishing the amount of light coming in, until he could finally see.

Everything was fluorescent and clean. He was walking down the middle of a busy hallway, his feet sliding across a shiny tiled floor. A gurney rolled past him, a tower with bags and tubes hanging down, pushed by two women in white shirts and pants. They quickly wheeled it around the corner. A man wearing a long white jacket over a blue shirt and tie passed him, carrying a clipboard that he studied. An elderly man in a hospital gown crept along, propping himself up with a tall portable stand hung with bags of medicine.

Then, just up ahead, Jonah saw something that caused him to stop suddenly. It was a figure moving like a shadow, unseen by anyone. It was wandering through the hallway, stopping at every patient it came across, leaning down in front of them, inspecting them. When it came to the elderly man, the shadow reached a hand out to touch his back. Jonah breathed in sharply as he saw the shadow's hand enter into the man, remain for a few seconds, then pull out again.

The shadow figure repeated this again and again down the hall, with every patient it came across. Jonah tried to follow it, but his legs were moving so slow. They felt as if they were locked in concrete. He needed to get to this creature. He knew the shadow was doing something evil, but he couldn't move fast enough.

Suddenly, the figure whipped its head around, looking back over its shoulder. Jonah knew instantly that it could see him. It seemed to consider for a few seconds whether to come for him. But it turned back, continuing its path down the hallway.

Before Jonah could think of what to do next, it had moved into the darkness at the end of the hall, and Jonah felt the light around him growing brighter again, until he couldn't see a thing.

༄

Jonah's eyes still closed, he replayed the dream in his mind again. It was so strange. Chasing a shadow creature down a hospital hallway . . . what did it mean?

That familiar whispering sound caused him to pop his eyes open. David was sitting up in bed, legs crossed and head bowed.

Jonah didn't waste any time. He entered the hidden realm as fast as he could.

David was there, the tendrils of light stretching up from his heart and through the ceiling as he prayed. Toward the door, a shadow lurked. But in the time it took for Jonah to blink and turn toward it, there was a flash of light. It split the shadow in two, turning it to dust.

What was that?

Then instantly, he knew.

The darkness of a fallen angel, the flash of an angelblade.

And as fast as that, it was only David again, continuing to pray.

Jonah left the hidden realm and watched quietly as David finished praying. He watched as his roommate struggled to push himself off the bed, rubbing his leg and moaning.

"You okay?" asked Jonah.

"My leg," David said, wincing. "It's still so sore." With a lot of effort, he pushed himself forward and sat on the edge of the bed.

Jonah tried to rub the sleep out of his eyes as he processed what he had just seen in the spiritual world. The weight of responsibility for his friend's injury fell heavily on his shoulders again though.

"I wish I could have that night back," Jonah said. "I'm sorry, David. I really am."

David's smile helped some of that burden to lift. "I know, Jonah," he said, rubbing his leg slowly. "I've already forgiven you. I was just praying about that, actually. I know I've been kind of cranky from the pain. But it's in the past, okay?"

Jonah rested his head on his pillow again. "Thanks."

Maybe Eliza and Julia would feel the same today too. He could only hope they would see things as David did. He shivered, wondering if the shadowy figures were trying to turn them against him too.

"Wonder what it would have been like if we didn't have Abigail's scarf?"

David thought about this. "Considering how you described me when I was out of it? I'm not sure I would be here right now. Apparently I looked like I was dead."

Jonah sat straight up in bed.

"What?" asked David.

He threw off the covers and quickly pulled on jeans and a long-sleeved T-shirt, his standard uniform since the sores had erupted. "Nothing," Jonah said. "I just had a good idea. See you at breakfast in a few."

Jonah put his shoes on and bounded through the door.

"See you there," David called out.

Jonah tried to ignore his headache as he hurried down the steps, even though every step he hit hurt. He wanted to make it before everyone arrived for breakfast.

When he arrived in the basement, he immediately found a round tray and set it beside the battered old latte maker the kids used to make coffee and tea when they were up late studying. After twenty minutes of pouring, he picked up his heavy tray, carefully balancing it as he walked back up the stairs. He had managed to get thirteen chai lattes onto the platter, and then moved slowly so he wouldn't spill a drop.

He timed it perfectly. As he rounded the corner to the dining hall, the quarterlings had just filed in and were beginning to fill their breakfast plates.

Jonah stood at the doorway with the trayful of steaming hot drinks.

"Hey, guys," he said. "I made us some drinks from downstairs. Thought everyone might like something warm this morning."

"Ooh, I needed one of those," Hai Ling said, stepping toward him. "I'm exhausted from yesterday."

"I'll take one," Andre said.

Rupert chimed in, "Me too."

Jonah smiled. Maybe a small effort like this was just what he needed to smooth over any tensions that were there.

"Thanks, Jonah," Julia said, even offering a small smile as she moved forward to grab one of the hot mugs.

Jonah moved toward them, ready to serve the drinks.

That's when he tripped. His feet locked together, stumbling over each other.

The first thing he heard was Hai Ling's shriek. Fumbling the tray, he tried to grab it back, then watched in slow motion as the mugs fell.

Milky brown tea filled the air, and neither Jonah, nor anyone else, had any power to stop it. It rained down onto the quarterlings just as the ceramic mugs shattered across the floor.

Everyone was screaming now as the hot liquid hit skin. Jonah just stood there, unable to believe what he had just done.

He thought he heard the faintest snickering laugh, but he was sure it hadn't come from any of the tea-soaked quarterlings in front of him. He looked all around, then back toward the door. It felt like someone had tripped him . . . but no one was there.

"Jonah!" Eliza yelled, frantically trying to brush the tea off her face and arms. "What were you thinking?"

"I'm burning! I'm burning!" Rupert shouted, grabbing a handful of napkins from the table to blot his face.

"What on earth is going on?"

They turned to see Sister Patricia standing in the doorway. She looked at the mugs on the floor and the kids covered in splotchy brown liquid. "Oh my goodness," she said, grabbing a huge stack of napkins and moving quickly to help them clean up.

Jonah just stood there as the chaos around him continued. Ruth was crying, along with Lania and Bridget. Hai Ling was screaming at him. Carlo seemed to have gotten the worst of it, the skin on his arms already blistering.

Jonah snapped out of his daze and grabbed a roll of paper towels to try to help. But no one wanted anything to do with him.

"Just get away from me!" Hai Ling screeched. "We don't need another injury around here."

"Back away, Stone," Frederick said, tending to his own wounds. "No one needs that kind of help."

He approached Julia, but even her face turned dark. "Not now, Jonah . . . I think you've done enough."

Jonah sighed, turned around, and walked out of the room to go shower before the next test.

He passed by Camilla's office in time to see the written exam scores, posted for all to see. Since they were listed alphabetically, he came to Eliza's and Jeremiah's before his.

Eliza Stone   100
Jeremiah Stone   86
Jonah Stone   63

"Unbelievable," he huffed. Things just kept getting worse and worse. Maybe someone would spear him during the morning's test and put him out of his misery.

⌘

At precisely ten o'clock, just as they had the day before, Camilla and the messenger angels appeared in the lobby. She immediately noticed the bandage on Carlo's arm.

"Carlo, what happened to you?" she asked, coming over to examine him. The quarterlings quickly relayed the story of Jonah and the tea as Jonah stood in the back, hanging his head. Camilla glanced at him, her eyes holding more compassion than annoyance.

"Remember, my friends, accidents do happen," she said, and then changed the subject, for which Jonah was grateful. "Are you prepared for another day of tests?"

The quarterlings responded with nods, but it was a more subdued reaction than yesterday.

"Today's test is archery. Frederick is at the top of the class so far," she said. The quarterlings applauded politely, and Frederick couldn't help but smile. "And very close behind is Eliza. Let me assure you, though, that the scores are very tight."

Before they could even ask her where they were going today, the messenger angels reached out, opened slivers of light in front of them, and they were gone. Jonah felt himself cracking like an egg, then he opened his eyes.

They were in the middle of a forest, with soaring trees above them, forming a green ceiling with specks of blue sky peeking through. The trees were old and thick, and some had trunks wider than the Stone family minivan.

"Where are we now?" asked Jeremiah, craning his neck up at all the trees.

"*Guten tag*, Jeremiah," Camilla responded. "We're in Germany.

The Black Forest, one of the most famous forests in the entire world."

"This sure smells better than New York," said Eliza, breathing in deeply as she studied a group of flowers nearby.

"Reminds me of Camilla's old garden," Jonah said.

"I was just thinking the same thing, Jonah!" called out the angel. "Now, if you will all follow me."

Jonah was surprised to see her walk up to the nearest tree and look up. Then she reached up and grabbed onto a set of rungs, invisible from farther away than ten feet. Jonah looked upward, into the trees, and saw a brown platform, positioned forty or fifty feet off the ground. It was just below the canopy formed by the tall trees.

Jeremiah saw it too. "It's like a tree house!" he said. "Do we get to go up there? And, Camilla, shouldn't you be flying?"

She laughed. "I haven't done this in . . . well, I've never done this. But there's a first time for everything." And with that, she began to climb the tree, beckoning the quarterlings to follow her.

"The angels installed this platform," she said as she climbed above them, "just for the test. Those not participating today should get a wonderful view from here."

"Don't look down, anyone," said Rupert as he peered wide-eyed to the ground below, which was getting farther and farther away. "We don't have the luxury of wings to catch us."

Of course, his comment only caused all of them to look down at the same time, and Carlo and Lania had twice as hard of a time climbing up after that.

Jonah pulled himself onto the platform after Camilla, then leaned over and helped each of the quarterlings. Using his angel strength, it didn't take much effort to snap them up beside him.

Although it bothered him when he noticed that a few of them hesitated to take his hand. Luckily, he didn't drop anyone.

Nathaniel emerged from behind a tree and landed on the platform.

"Welcome! Are you ready for your next test?" he said. They responded with enthusiastic applause. "It sounds like you are," he continued. "Today, my friends, we are in the Black Forest in Germany, one of the most beautiful forests on Elohim's earth, where some of you will take your midterm in Angelic Archery.

"The rules are very simple," Nathaniel continued. "Shoot at any target that poses a legitimate threat. We'll be judging you on speed, accuracy, and number of hits. As you found out yesterday, you won't be shooting at a bull's-eye on a wall. Your targets will be a little more mobile than that."

He said this with a twinkle in his eye.

"The arrows you are using today have special tips," Camilla said. "It's kind of like having the safety on. They hit their targets and stick, but they don't hurt anyone."

It was just the quarterlings with the gift of archery today—David, Jonah, Frederick, Hai Ling, and Lania.

"All of you with the gift of archery, are you ready?" Camilla asked, then looked at David with compassion. "David, my dear, we are going to ask that, because of your injury in the confrontation with those beasts, you sit out again today. I am sorry. It is simply too much of a risk for you on that leg."

David looked dejected, and for a second Jonah thought he might protest, but instead he nodded his head, staring at the ground.

"Sorry, David," Jonah whispered. David nodded and then looked down again, rubbing his leg.

Jonah felt awful. He knew how much David wanted to compete, and now he couldn't. And it was all Jonah's fault.

"Just do your best," Camilla reminded them. "We'll be overhead, tracking what's happening and grading you. The main thing now, archers, is to give Elohim your best. And all I can tell you is to keep your eyes alert at all times and try to stay calm."

Angels flew over, landing behind them. Jonah was surprised to see Henry, his old guardian angel, waiting for him.

"Henry!" he said, high-fiving him and giving him a hug. "I didn't know you were going to be here. It's nice to see a friendly face." Jonah said this as he glanced around at the other quarterlings.

Henry, who still looked like a teenager even though he was covered with armor, gave Jonah his usual smile. "You're going to do great, Jonah. Just remember everything I taught you." He winked at him and extended his arm.

Jonah and the others floated downward on the arms of the angels. As Jonah did, he suddenly felt dizzy. His head seemed to be spinning around, and his vision grew blurry. He blinked for a few seconds, rubbing his eyes, unable to bring things into focus. Shaking his head to the side, his eyes finally adjusted back to normal again.

"Are you okay, Jonah?"

Jonah saw the concern on Henry's face as they landed in the middle of the clearing with the others.

"Yeah, I'm good," he said uneasily, blinking a few more times. "Just got dizzy for a sec, but all better now. Must have been the change in elevation on the flight down or something."

Henry smiled. "All right, then. May Elohim bless you, Jonah."

The angels darted off, leaving the quarterlings standing back-to-back on the forest floor. Jonah felt his pulse quicken and his breathing grow sharper. He tried to remind himself that this was just a test. He needed to stay calm and focused.

But his mind buzzed with images of David in the museum the other night, the awful wound on his leg, and then his face up on the platform. He looked upward and saw David standing among the other quarterlings, his hand raised. He was cheering Jonah on! Just knowing that made things easier.

Jonah snapped his head back down and found that his breathing began to slow. Just in time, too, because as he watched the forest in front of him, he suddenly saw movement. His arm naturally went behind his back and grabbed an arrow. The bow formed in his left hand, and he strung it, ready to let it rip when the time was right.

The forest exploded with action. One fallen angel crossed in front of him on his left, moving from tree to tree. Then another snuck out on his right, emerging to fire one of his own arrows directly at Jonah.

His instincts took over. He rolled onto the ground, ducking the arrow by only a few inches. Still holding his own arrow, he aimed and let it go. The flaming arrow made a line for the fallen angel and was true to its aim. It hit him in the chest, and the angel fell.

Jonah began to move faster now, away from the unshielded center of the forest and into the trees. He knew that he couldn't stay in one place for long. His chances would be much better if he kept moving. Another of the dark creatures emerged to his left, jumping up from behind a large log on the ground. Jonah turned and fired, hitting the creature in the neck.

Keep moving, Jonah. Keep going until the horn blows. He told himself this over and over as he continued to make quick work of the opposition. He lost count after hitting six.

A flame flashed in his vision to his left, and he slammed his chest down on the ground. The sharp point of an arrow stuck into the tree just above his head, red flame burning. *I hope that wouldn't have actually hurt me if I'd been hit,* he thought. But the tip looked sharp.

Another one came, and he ducked again. This one hit even lower on the tree. Jonah was starting to get mad.

He searched the green wall of trees and plants in front of him, but he couldn't spot the fallen angel. His position on the ground wasn't helping him. Studying the tree he was leaning up against, he decided to make a move.

Jumping up, he used his angel strength to leap upward to the first hanging branch. Quickly he began to scale the tree, moving from branch to branch until he was halfway up the giant elm. He found a large limb and crouched down. Now he had a view of the entire floor. He could see not only several fallen angels, but also the other quarterlings.

He spotted the fallen angel behind a bush, likely the one who had fired at him, and he reached back for an arrow. As he did, though, the one fallen angel turned into two. Jonah blinked. Did that just happen?

Except that it wasn't just two fallen angels . . . it was two of everything. Two bushes, two trees, and two Fredericks, just below him, firing two arrows. His vision was blurring again. And his head was beginning to feel light. Reaching down, he grabbed onto the branch he was kneeling on to steady himself. He let go of the arrow, and it dropped harmlessly to the forest floor.

Jonah looked down. He could barely see his hand, let alone anything below. With his other hand, he rubbed his eyes, trying to get his vision to return.

But then he lost his balance, teetering on the branch for a moment before he began to fall.

Which is when everything turned black.

∽

Jonah heard the voice of someone far off in the distance. It was difficult to make out the words, but it sounded as if someone were praying.

"Elohim, we ask that You bring healing to Jonah now, that if it is in Your will, You allow him to be free from injury, that You bring him close to Yourself . . ."

He fluttered his eyes open. All he could see were blobs of light, and then some darker shadows over him. He heard more words murmured that he couldn't make out. His back hurt. His legs and arms hurt. His entire body was in pain. Jonah tried to raise his head up and say something, but blackness overtook him again, and he lost sight of everything.

FIFTEEN

A NEW ENEMY

Yes, the testing is on hold for the quarterlings until we can be sure of their safety."

Jonah recognized the voice of Camilla ringing in his ears. He was trying to see her, trying to open up his eyes, but all he could see in front of him was hazy darkness. Where was he?

"These wounds on his arms and legs, they concern me," another voice said, one that he knew as well. Was that Taryn? "My feeling is that these and his fall are related."

"Yes," came Camilla's voice again, sounding tired and old. "They are. But there is nothing we can do about that right now. Elohim has a plan, and we will just have to see it through. The best we can hope for is to keep him and the other quarterlings as safe as we can." She paused. "As much as that is possible at this point. We should have just stuck to written tests . . ."

A gruff voice, which Jonah immediately knew belonged to Marcus, entered the conversation, speaking low. "I think we all know what is going on here, don't we, Camilla? The boils all over him that won't be healed by human medicine? They clearly have come from M'chala himself, and I am not going—"

"Enough!" Camilla cut him off. "Enough, Marcus. I am not disagreeing with you, but it is not ours right now to meddle with! We are not to interfere."

Jonah began to move his eyelids. Finally, and with a lot of effort, he pried them open. Above him, Camilla, Marcus, and Taryn stood, peering down at him.

"Interfere with what?" he said sleepily, their words swimming around in his head.

Camilla gave a quick glance toward Marcus and Taryn. "Jonah!" she said, now leaning over him and touching his forehead. "You're back with us. Thanks to Elohim!"

He nodded, still a little groggy, but as he looked up, at least he could see clearly now. His whole body ached, but he gradually raised himself so he was sitting on the edge of the bed.

"Careful now, Jonah," said Taryn, holding his elbow. "You took a nasty fall out there. It's a wonder you didn't break anything."

The fall. He remembered it now, wincing again at the thought of it. Looking around the room, he saw a desk, a stack of books, and a stained glass window that he recognized as being from the convent.

"Camilla's office?"

Camilla nodded. "You've been resting here for a couple of hours now."

Jonah rubbed his arm, which was tender. "Did I pass the exam?"

"The exam," answered Camilla, sighing loudly. "We're considering cancelling the exams at this point. After what happened to you . . ."

"You should keep it going," Jonah said. "We've all worked really hard. I just got a little dizzy and fell, that's all. And that could happen in the real world. We all need to be prepared. We need to know how to handle things if one of us gets injured fighting. We need to know how to take care of each other."

She looked at him, and Jonah had the distinct feeling that she wanted to tell him something more, but decided against it. "We'll see about that," was all she said, turning back toward her window.

"Frederick had the highest score when you fell," Marcus said softly so Camilla couldn't hear. "But you did hit eight before you plummeted to the ground. You did well."

Jonah tried to read into his eyes for a few seconds, to see if there was anything else there. Marcus stepped away, though, lowering his head.

"Marcus," Jonah asked, beckoning him back. "Who is M'chala?"

The smile drifted from the angel's face. He batted away the question. "You need to get back to your room now and rest. We'll regroup tomorrow. Okay?"

Marcus and Taryn both tried to help him stand up.

"I'd like for you to speak with your parents before you go upstairs," Taryn said. "I know they're going to want to talk to you and see that you are okay."

Jonah agreed, and they walked through the convent doors and onto the sidewalk. Taryn raised her arms and concentrated, and soon they were surrounded by an Angelic Vortex. Within seconds, the screen in front of them appeared, and his parents' concerned faces were peering at Jonah inside the cyclone.

"Jonah!" Benjamin said. "Henry brought us up to speed on your accident. How are you feeling?"

Jonah shrugged. "Not all that great, I guess. But I'm okay. It was just a little fall."

Eleanor leaned in closer and tried to speak but coughed. It

took her a minute to get herself together, still hacking in between her words. "A fall . . . of forty . . . feet? That's not . . . little."

"I'm sore," he conceded. "I did get light-headed up there. But I feel better now. Really. I didn't eat any breakfast before the competition. It was probably just low blood sugar. I'll make sure to eat before my next test." He didn't want them to worry and was doing his best to convince them not to.

"Well," his father said, "you just need to be more careful, okay, Jonah? But we're glad to see that you're all right. Even though, honestly, the sores look worse."

Jonah glanced down at his arms, feeling the sudden urge to itch them. He ignored his dad's comment. "Mom, are you okay? You don't look any better than when I saw you last."

Benjamin cut his eyes toward her. "She's seeing some doctors here in Peacefield," he said, but remained tight-lipped. "But nothing for you to worry about right now."

She was coughing again, unable to speak, but nodded in agreement with Benjamin.

"Okay . . . if you say so," Jonah said slowly, knowing in his heart that they weren't telling him everything. She looked at him with her heavy eyes and tried to smile.

They said their good-byes and the vortex was gone.

"She doesn't look good," Jonah said to Taryn.

Taryn gazed at the street beside them. "You're right. I don't know what is going on with her. But she is in good hands. Now let me help you get back upstairs."

Jonah shuffled toward the door. "I'm good," he said, waving his hand. "Just going to go get some rest." He thanked her as he moved his sore body back into the corridor toward his room.

"Jonah!"

He almost didn't turn around at the sound of his brother's voice, calling to him from down the hallway.

"Jonah, wait!"

Jeremiah was barreling toward him, causing Jonah to flinch. The last thing he wanted was to end up flat on his back again. But instead, his brother stopped right in front of him and studied him up and down.

"Well, you look better than you did a while ago," he said. "I thought you might have broken your legs or something."

Jonah sighed, turning to go. "No, Jeremiah. I guess I got lucky and didn't break anything. Although I bet everyone around here wishes I had right now."

Jeremiah crossed his arms. "I don't. And anyone who says anything like that will have to deal with me."

Jonah couldn't help but smile at the thought of one of the smallest kids here going up against someone like Frederick or Andre.

"Thanks, Jeremiah," he said, slapping a high five with his brother. "You may be the only one who feels like that right now."

"Yeah, I know," Jeremiah said. "But Dad says brothers have to stick together. Right?"

Jonah punched him playfully in the arm. "Right."

Stepping into the bathroom across the hallway, Jonah stopped in front of the mirror. His shaggy hair was matted down, extra greasy from the sweat of the competition and the lack of a shower. His entire body was red with the boils, and his dad was right—they only seemed to be getting worse. He desperately wanted to scratch them, but he knew if he did, it would only make them worse. His head pounded as he leaned over the sink, running the water and splashing it on his face.

He had never looked, or felt, more awful.

But that word lingered in his mind.

M'chala.

What did that mean?

His body longed to be in bed, but his legs took him in a different direction. Down the hallway and down the long steps into the basement room. He didn't want to ask any of the angels about it, and he didn't figure Eliza or any of his friends would be speaking to him yet. But at least he could do a little research himself.

He limped across the floor and plopped himself down in front of a desktop computer sitting on a corner desk.

He shook the mouse, and the screen came to life. He knew an Internet search was a long shot, but at least it would be a good place to start.

He tried to spell it every way he could think of. Nothing came up that was interesting in the search results. He scanned page after page of returns, and was about to click off the screen when something caught his eye.

An obscure result from some type of Hebrew dictionary. *Where's Eliza when I need her?* He would have to navigate the details himself. A Hebrew word popped up: MACHALAH.

He read the entry out loud. "The definition of MACHALAH in Hebrew is . . . sickness or disease."

Jonah leaned back in his chair, his mind racing now. Standing up, he picked up a basketball and began to dribble it around. Back in Peacefield, shooting hoops outside of his house always calmed him down and helped him think.

How did the dictionary information fit in with what he heard from Marcus? It was as if the angel was talking about *someone,* not just a random illness.

Another thought sparked in his mind. Hurrying back over to the computer, he typed in another search:

SICKNESS AND DISEASE IN THE NEW TESTAMENT

He scanned through the list of illnesses that came up, making mental notes as he went along. Some people Jesus came across were suffering from regular sicknesses that often plagued humans. Other times, it seemed that Jesus knew there was an actual fallen angel tormenting the person. He commanded them to leave, and they did immediately.

Jonah's mind suddenly drifted back to his most recent dream. The shadowy figure walking down the hospital hallway, touching the sick . . . Could it be? Could it have been a prophecy dream?

He glanced up at the wall of ancient books to his left. He knew that Eliza had been reading them in her spare time, but he had yet to crack one. *Maybe I should have before now.*

"M'chala," he said to himself as he read the titles of the books. "Where are you?" He looked in the *M* section first. Nothing there. *That would have been way too easy.*

Fingering the books as he walked along, he saw ancient commentaries on books of the Bible, a book all about the Archangel Michael, and a large tome dedicated to angelic weaponry. *I'll have to check that out sometime*, he thought to himself.

He stopped in front of one crusty leather book the angels had given them to help them study: *The Angelic Encyclopedia of Angels, the Fallen, and Other Creatures of the Hidden Realm.*

"Maybe . . . ," he whispered, pulling the dusty book from the shelf and placing it gently onto a table.

He paged through it, careful to turn the dusty pages so they didn't rip. He passed by pictures of angels, fallen angels, and all sorts of monsters, with descriptions written about each.

He found a section with a large scrolled *M* at the top of the page. He flipped through the next few pages until he found one that read, "M'chala, the fallen angel of disease and sickness" at the top. There was a picture frame for him, but no image of the creature—it was only a black square.

The rest of the page was empty. No information, no details, nothing.

He closed the book slowly.

M'chala, the one in charge of sickness, was the one afflicting Jonah. He was sure of it. No wonder there was no picture there. All he remembered from his dream was a dark shadow.

But his affliction now had a cause, and somehow, as awful as this creature must be, Jonah began to feel more focused.

If M'chala was responsible, Jonah had to find him. Before the Fallen harmed him again. And before the Fallen hurt anyone else around him.

Or worse.

PART III

INTO THE SHADOWS

Though He slay me,

yet will I trust Him.

Job 13:15 NKJV

SIXTEEN

SPEED AND STRENGTH

W here are we this time?" Jeremiah asked after the messenger angels dropped them off for that day's test.

Jonah looked up to see that ancient stone surrounded the quarterlings. They were standing on a circular dirt area, with a stadium of bleachers made from rock all around. Columns were visible above the seats, most of them chipped off and broken.

"This looks like . . . ," David said.

"The Roman Coliseum!" Eliza said, her excitement evident in her voice.

They were standing in the middle of the arena, and they all took a minute to survey the scene. Jonah remembered from history class, and more than a few movies he'd watched with his dad, that this was where the gladiators fought in ancient Rome.

"Nice place, Camilla," Jonah said. "So we're going to compete here today?"

"We thought it might be a nice reminder of what these examinations are all about," she said. "Many men lost their lives here, but remember, our fight is not with flesh and blood, but against a much more dangerous—and deadly—opponent: Abaddon himself. Remember today that this is why we are testing you. Not for grades or to determine who is at the head of the class, but so that you are prepared to fight against Abaddon and his army—no matter the cost."

"Today," Nathaniel broke in, "there will be more testing of your unique gifts. The sandals of speed, angelic strength, the breastplate of righteousness, the helmet of salvation . . . and even the sword of the Spirit." He nodded at Jonah, who was the only one possessing an angelblade. "We know that some of these gifts are held by only one person. No matter. As we've already said, you will be measured by your ability with your own gifts, not by the gifts of others."

He outlined how the day would go, and they split into different groups. Jonah would be tested on the sandals of speed and angelic strength. He was determined to put everything he had discovered about M'chala out of his mind, at least for now, and focus on the exams.

Around the outer edges, closest to the stone bleachers, a track was laid out. He and the other runners were called over: Frederick, Hai Ling, Lania, and David. David was still walking with a limp.

"Are you sure you can do this, David?" he asked his friend as they made their way to the starting line.

"I'm going to try," he said with as much cheer as he could muster. "What about you, though? It was only yesterday that I recall you were falling from a tree, Jonah."

Jonah did feel sore this morning, but he had been able to shake it off. "I'm just really lucky, I guess. No broken bones, just a little stiff when I woke up. The prayers seemed to really help."

Jonah really wanted to tell David about his research last night, about the name he had overheard from the angels, about the monster that was out there. He opened his mouth, but then shut it again.

"What is it, Jonah?" David asked, trying to read his friend's face.

Jonah shook his head. He couldn't pull his friend into something dangerous again, especially since they were barely on speaking terms. "I just wanted to say . . . I hope you do well today. And I'm really sorry about your leg."

"Oh, okay," David said. "I told you to forget about that already, though. Now let's go race."

The test would be simple. They had to complete seven laps as fast as they could. The first to finish would, obviously, get the highest marks. Jonah looked into the faces of his opponents, and he felt the tension rise into his shoulders. Frederick wouldn't even look at Jonah. He had already toed the starting line, looking straight ahead, waiting for the gun to go off.

Nathaniel, who was observing all of the quarterlings as they found their different sections of the arena, came over to watch the start. All of the runners stepped up to the line beside Frederick. Jonah found himself with Hai Ling to his left and Frederick on his right. Lania and David took the outside slots.

"Racers!" Taryn called out, holding up her hands. "Prepare your feet for the race!"

They each bowed their heads, and their shoes disappeared. Brown sandals took their place. Jonah picked his feet up, slapping the bottoms of them with his hands. They felt light and fast. He was ready.

Taryn held her hands apart as they knelt down. "Seven laps, my friends. The fastest one gets top marks."

The other quarterlings stopped for a minute and turned their attention to the track.

"On your marks!"

Jonah breathed in deeply, focusing on the track in front of him.

Taryn brought her hands together in a clap, but it sounded like a thunderous bang.

He lurched forward, pushing his legs into the dirt, slipping a little but pressing ahead. Sensing Frederick and Hai Ling beside him, hearing their footsteps and their deep breaths, he knew they were even.

A curve in the track was ahead, and Jonah knew that if he could press harder into it, he could gain an advantage. He bore down and leaned into the turn. As soon as he tried to dig his right foot into the dirt, though, it slipped.

With all the speed he had generated, there was no way to regain control. He found himself flying through the air. Frederick jumped, timing it perfectly so that he flew right over Jonah. He just missed Lania, who was a couple of steps behind. He slid on his chest across the dirt, almost hitting a rock wall at the edge of the track.

"Gaaaaaaaahhhhh!" he yelled, slamming his hand down on the dirt and pushing himself back up. The dust from the track had been kicked up, but through it he could see the other four runners moving as fast as they could away from him.

Jonah jumped back on the track, finding himself almost half of a lap down to Frederick, who had taken a commanding lead.

"Come on, come on," he growled, starting to run again. There was so much distance between them, though, that Jonah couldn't see how he would be able to make it up. His feet were back up to speed, and soon he was at least keeping up with them again. He could see Frederick out of the corner of his eye, burning ahead of the others.

He may not be able to win, but he could put up a good challenge at least. Jonah found himself beginning to utter short, quick prayers.

"Please..."

"Help me..."

"Go faster..."

He felt his feet churning faster and faster, but he kept his focus on the path about ten feet ahead, not even willing to look up yet. He continued to pray as he passed the start line again. Six more laps to go.

He found himself letting go, allowing his mind to focus on Elohim and his feet to do the work. All the while he didn't look up. Before he knew it, he had finished another lap. And then another. Four left.

Then three.

And then, as his legs began to hurt, he crossed the line once again. Only two to go. For the first time, another runner came into his vision. His friend David, struggling around the track, was just up ahead now. The lanky African's leg was giving out, and even though Jonah could tell David was giving it all he had, it just wasn't enough. He moved past him in a flash.

The pain in his leg muscles was growing, but he knew it was probably there for everyone. What was more, he had spotted Lania not that far ahead of him.

I must be moving pretty fast, he thought to himself. *Just keep pushing, Jonah, keep going...*

Soon, he was passing Lania, who had run out of breath and seemed on the verge of quitting.

"Keep it up," he huffed as he passed. "Keep going!"

He moved past her, just as he crossed the line again. One lap left.

"Come on . . ."

"Let me . . ."

"Keep going . . ."

He peeked up and, to his surprise, saw Hai Ling blazing just in front of him. And up ahead of her, Frederick, running faster than Jonah had ever seen. But Jonah found himself gaining, somehow, on them both.

Halfway around, he passed Hai Ling, who screeched loudly in frustration when she saw him.

"Don't quit, Hai Ling! Come on!" he yelled out to her as he passed.

She must have heard him because she sped up again, almost pulling even with Jonah before he dug even deeper. Frederick was within his sights now, and he felt the pain in his legs disappear.

It wasn't until the last fifty feet of the race that Jonah realized he was not going to win. Frederick was too fast, too determined. He looked back over his shoulder, gave Jonah a satisfied smile, and thrust himself even faster toward the finish line. He crossed it with Jonah five steps behind.

They rested on their knees, sucking in air as fast as they could. Frederick then stood tall and raised one hand in the air as he walked back toward the others.

"Nice run, Frederick," Jonah muttered as he walked past.

"You too," he replied. "You made up some ground there pretty fast. If it wasn't for that slip . . ." He slammed his hand down on Jonah's shoulder and went to talk to Hai Ling and Lania.

I'm sure he's telling them how great he was, Jonah thought as he spit into the dust at his feet.

He stood and watched the other quarterlings being tested in the middle of the arena for a while. Eliza was with Rupert, Julia, Bridget, and Carlo, who all had their shields of faith raised as spheres the size of bowling balls were being launched at them from all directions. The brightness of some of the shields was fading as they got hit, but Jonah wasn't surprised to see that Eliza's was holding steady.

Jeremiah was being tested in his use of the breastplate of righteousness in another corner of the stadium. The exam consisted of a number of disguised angels charging him from different positions, and him trying to fend them off by calling on the armor. Jonah couldn't hear him from where he was, but he saw the blasts from the breastplate and knew that his brother was declaring truths of Elohim, which gave his weapon its power.

"All those quarterlings participating in the angelic strength event, please come and join me here!"

Jonah heard the booming announcement from Marcus and found him standing at the tallest point of the arena, up above the bleachers, underneath a set of columns. He tried to keep from rolling his eyes as he saw Frederick walking ahead of him. He would have to face him in this competition too.

Andre, Lania, and Ruth were standing with Marcus when Jonah arrived. They were surrounded by columns of marble, some standing, others having fallen to the ground thousands of years ago. There was a wide path, a walkway, in between the rows of columns still erect. On the ground were five of the large cylinders of stone, all the same size.

Taryn stood down the path in front of them, Jonah guessed the length of a football field away. She waved at them, and the quarterlings waved back.

"Your goal," Marcus said, "is to lift one of the columns and carry it to Taryn. The one who arrives first gets the most points."

Jonah smiled to himself. *This shouldn't be a problem at all.* But he eyed Andre, the enormous Russian, who was stretching and flexing his muscles and grunting loudly, and he felt his confidence erode just a little.

"Are you ready for this, Ruth?" he asked as she stared down at the column. She was tall but slender, and he wondered how she would possibly be able to lift the heavy weight.

She smiled up at him. "I believe I am ready," she said without a hint of worry. Jonah nodded, impressed with her attitude.

"Just what I would expect to hear from David's sister," he said, causing her to break into a wide grin.

He lined up beside Frederick again, with Ruth to his left. Andre and Lania were on the outside lanes.

"Looks like it's you and me fighting for it again, Stone," Frederick said, with his usual overconfident smile.

"I don't know," Jonah said, looking over at Andre, who had grown very intense. "If I were you, I'd watch out for the big Russian down there."

Marcus waited until they were settled, with their arms around the columns at their feet. Just like Taryn had done, he raised his arms and clapped loudly, signaling the beginning of the race.

Jonah strained to pick up the stone column at his feet. It was heavier than he thought. He grunted and got down low to the ground, finally getting some movement from the heavy rock. Glancing toward the others, he saw they were having as much trouble as he was. All of them except for Andre, at least. He had already picked up the column and placed it on his shoulder as if it were a giant bag of marshmallows.

"What's wrong, guys?" he called back to them as he bounded toward Taryn. "Too heavy for you?" They heard his laughter fade in the distance.

Jonah bear-hugged the column and began to move. Frederick had picked his up at the same time, and to Jonah's surprise, so had Ruth. Lania was well behind, struggling to get her arms around it.

Jonah quickly found that balance was more important than speed. Several times he found himself going too fast and fell forward, dropping the column on the ground and having to pick it back up again. Frederick was having the same struggle. Ruth, on the other hand, was coolly walking ahead at an unrushed pace and hadn't dropped hers yet.

Halfway through the contest, Jonah saw Andre cross the finish line beside Taryn and toss his weight to the ground. Frederick was beside him, inching ahead, though, while Ruth held second place all to herself. Jonah felt his legs growing tired again but tried to push through. Every time he attempted to move faster, though, he ended up dropping the column in front of him.

Frederick was struggling with the same thing. But he was still ahead.

Jonah cried out in frustration and grabbed the column again, rushing forward as fast as he could. There was no way he was going to let Frederick beat him again, no matter what happened.

He was twenty feet from the finish line when he lost his balance. This time, though, his legs were moving so fast that when the column fell, he found himself underneath it. The only things that saved his head from being crushed were his hands, holding the heavy marble inches away from his face. It was sitting on top of him, and he was starting to have a hard time breathing.

Suddenly the column began to move. It was lifted off him and thrown to the side. Andre and Marcus stood over him.

"Jonah? Are you all right?" Andre asked, his brow wrinkled with concern. "It didn't crush you, did it?"

Jonah sat up and slapped his hand on the ground. "I'm all right," he said. "Just lost my balance, that's all." He watched as Lania crossed the finish line. "I guess that means I'm last."

Marcus nodded but didn't say anything. Jonah dropped himself down on his back again, staring upward at the cloudy sky. He didn't want to see anyone. Not Andre, Frederick, or anyone else. All he wanted was to be left alone.

SEVENTEEN

A DANGEROUS PLAN

The quarterlings were rowdy as the messenger angels were preparing to transport them back to the convent for the evening. All except Jonah, who stood off to the side, occasionally kicking at the dirt with his sneaker. The results had been tabulated, all scores being taken into account. The leaders were announced by Nathaniel:

> *First Place: Frederick*
> *Second Place: Eliza*
> *Third Place: Jonah*

Jonah was behind with only one event left—the battle simulation. Anything was possible, but it seemed highly unlikely that he could catch Frederick now, especially with how well the South African was performing.

Jonah felt sick—his head throbbed, he felt shaky and tired, and his skin hurt. His poor performance definitely didn't make him feel any better. Carlo still had bandages on his arms, which reminded Jonah of the incident with the tea. Nothing was going right. He couldn't blame his friends for avoiding him—he wouldn't want to be around himself either, especially after how the last few days had gone. He seemed to be bringing bad luck with him everywhere he went.

Jonah rushed back to his room, ignoring Eliza's voice calling after him in the hallway. He didn't want to talk right now. And he certainly didn't want to get anyone else hurt.

Flopping facedown on the mattress, he prayed that he could develop a new gift—invisibility. Then nobody would have to see him ever again.

Instead, he found his mind drifting back to his dream from the other night and the research he had done. The image from the book kept coming to him, the sparse page with an empty black box and the word *M'chala* written above. He twirled it over and over in his mind. At one point, he tried to forget it. What could he possibly do? But the image from his dream wouldn't let him alone.

He was facing the wall, lying on his stomach, when he heard David come in.

"Jonah?" he said softly. Jonah didn't move. "Jonah, aren't you going to eat dinner? They're closing the kitchen down."

But Jonah remained motionless, pretending to be asleep. He simply couldn't face his roommate right now, not after the embarrassment of today. He also had decided what he was going to do tonight. What he needed to do. And he couldn't risk having David involved.

Jonah waited until David climbed into bed and he heard his steady, slow breathing so that he knew he was asleep. He sat up on the edge of his bed, watching David for a few minutes to make sure.

He hopped up and opened his top drawer. What he needed now was the MissionFinder 3000, the watch he had been given by Marcus that had helped him so much in his adventures in the past. He hoped it would give him some clue of where to go.

But he couldn't find it. He searched through his socks and underwear, but it wasn't there. Neither was it in any of his other drawers or his book bag. Soon, he had quietly searched the whole room.

"Great," he mumbled. "What is it going to be next, Jonah? You going to accidentally set the building on fire?"

He stood for a few seconds, wondering what to do. One possibility was to crawl back into bed and call it a night. He rubbed the painful boils on his arms, thinking about how good it would feel to just fall asleep and start over in the morning. The alternative was dangerous and unclear.

But maybe M'chala was somehow the key, and if he could only locate him . . .

That was the information he was hoping to find in the MissionFinder, though. How could he find him without it?

Jonah was about to crawl back into bed when an idea hit him. He wasn't sure it would work, but it was worth a shot.

✳

An hour later, after sneaking through the back door of the convent, moving as quickly and quietly as he could, hoping to avoid detection from both the angels and any fallen ones who might be lurking about, he stood in front of the building. Wind was whipping off the East River, not too far away, bringing a chill and, along with it, the faint smell of garbage.

The sign before him read BELLEVUE HOSPITAL CENTER. He had looked it up on the Internet map before he left, and it was the closest large hospital to him. There was a reason he had seen M'chala in a hospital in his dream. If this was the fallen angel in charge of sickness and disease, didn't it make sense that he would be hiding out in a hospital?

Two security guards were standing by the double-door entrance. Jonah stuffed his hands in his pockets, pulled his hood off his head, and walked toward them. *Just act like you belong here, Jonah. They won't say anything.*

"Can I help you, son?" Jonah couldn't see the guard's mouth move because of his enormous mustache. The guard studied his face for a few seconds. "Do you need to see a doctor?"

He tried to smile. "No, I'm . . . uh . . . here to see a friend." Jonah reached for the door handle, but the guard stepped in front of him.

"It's just past eleven o'clock," he said, crossing his arms. "Visiting hours are long over. Who is it that you need to see?"

Jonah stood in front of him for a few seconds, mouth hanging open, trying to decide what to do. He could make up a story, go into a long tale about a dying aunt who was having surgery or a nephew who had just been born, but he didn't feel great about lying to a security officer. And he wasn't good at it anyway. *How about the hidden realm, genius?* He laughed at himself, realizing he'd forgotten the easiest way to get in.

"Something funny?" The other officer stepped forward now, placing his hand on the end of his billy club.

"Funny? No, no," Jonah said. "I didn't mean to laugh . . . I was just thinking about something else." He backed up, putting his hands up. "Sorry, officers. I didn't realize how late it had gotten.

I'll just call them, how about that?" They grunted their approval, and Jonah walked away, waving back at them.

Less than a minute later, he walked right past the guards, sliding the door open just enough to get through.

"Darn wind!" he heard one of the officers say, pulling the door shut behind him.

Jonah walked across the lobby of the hospital. A long desk was along one wall, with two attendants stationed there, both on the phone while staring at their computers. A bank of escalators was on their right.

He wasn't sure where to go from here, but the escalators looked like a good start. Hopping on the first step, he let it carry him upward as he studied the nondescript paintings of flower arrangements hung neatly along the wall. When he stepped off on the second floor, he found himself in front of a bank of elevators.

Jonah studied the sign on the wall, which listed all of the different medical departments and on what floor they were located. There were more than a dozen, from pediatrics to oncology to the heart center. *If I were M'chala, the fallen angel in charge of disease, where would I go?* He shivered, not enjoying putting himself in that fallen one's shoes. But as he looked harder at the list, his eyes fell on one floor in particular.

"Intensive Care Unit, Floor 9," he said under his breath. "As good a place as any to start looking."

He followed a young man in a white jacket with a stethoscope draped around his neck onto the elevator. The man pushed the button for the tenth floor and began studying a clipboard full of notes.

Jonah, still in the hidden realm, slid around him and, eyeing him to make sure he was still looking down, pressed button number nine.

When the elevator arrived, the doctor walked off right after Jonah.

"Wait . . . what?" he said, confused for a second, before reaching back and grabbing the closing door and jumping back in. "That was strange," Jonah heard him say as the doors shut.

Jonah took a deep breath as he walked down the hallway of the intensive care unit. He glanced in the first room he came to, unprepared for what he saw. An older woman was lying in a bed, an oxygen mask on her face, with what seemed like more than a dozen tubes coming out of her. Machines surrounded her, blinking and beeping in the darkened room. She didn't move, but the steady beep of the heart rate monitor told him she was still alive.

These people are in the worst condition of anyone in the hospital, he thought. *Stay focused, Jonah. M'chala could be anywhere in here.*

He moved on, passing by other rooms, people hooked up to machines and lying in beds, unmoving. He stopped in front of a room where a teenage boy was asleep, breathing through his mask. His parents stood over him, looks of worry creasing their faces as they spoke soft words to him and each other. The boy had brown, unkempt hair, and his feet stretched off the end of the bed.

That could be me.

He watched for another minute as the boy's mom pressed her hand against her forehead and the boy's dad stood over her, rubbing her shoulders. They were so worried.

Jonah stepped quietly into the room. He needed to get a closer look. Moving over to the other side of the bed, he tried to get a glimpse of his chest underneath the covers. He breathed out a sigh as he saw the glow he had been looking for. This one was a child of Elohim. He had placed himself in His hands. Jonah nodded, even praying a silent prayer for the boy.

The stark white hallway was quiet, except for the footsteps of an occasional nurse or doctor. He was almost to the end when he saw something that made him freeze.

A greenish shadowy haze moved into the hallway from the last room and began to gather together in front of him, forming something. The hallway grew darker as the image of a face came into view. A torso, legs, and finally, wings.

"M'chala," Jonah said, barely above a whisper. His hand automatically moved to his hip, ready to pull his angelblade at any moment.

"Jonah Stone, what a nice surprise," the fallen angel seethed. "What brings you to the hospital? You know this is my territory, don't you?"

Jonah swallowed hard, looking up at the green face. He was taller than any fallen angel he had ever seen and extremely thin. His head skimmed along the ceiling.

"I believe I found who I'm looking for," he said, summoning his most courageous voice.

The fallen angel raised his eyebrows, studying the quarterling for a few seconds. "Have you enjoyed what I did to your skin?" he jeered. "Tell me, Jonah, how's it been between you and the ladies since you've become the most pimpled kid in the world?"

The reality hit Jonah like a blow to the stomach. M'chala was the one responsible for his sores. Then images of Eliza, Julia, and David flashed through his mind. And his mother—she was sick too. He fumed, pulling out his angelblade and holding it between them. Light from the blade eclipsed the darkened hall.

"I don't care about this," Jonah said, holding up his left arm. "Do it all you want! But you need to leave my family and my friends out of it!"

He surprised himself with the boldness that came out of his mouth. He was, after all, face-to-face with the fallen angel responsible for all sickness and disease.

"You really want that, Jonah?"

M'chala moved closer to Jonah now, pointing his long, crooked finger toward the boy. Jonah held his blade with both hands, mainly to try to keep it from shaking. He watched the tip of M'chala's finger, wondering what kind of disease awaited him if he touched his body.

"I told you," Jonah said, still focusing on the finger. "If you're the one causing all of this trouble with my family and friends, it needs to stop. You can do whatever you want with me."

Jonah shifted his gaze from M'chala's finger to his green eyes and slowly began to lower his blade. M'chala glared at him with the look of an animal who'd just cornered its prey.

He drew his finger closer and closer, until it was an inch away from Jonah's nose. Jonah stood still, waiting for a strike from the fallen angel, and closed his eyes.

For what seemed like minutes dripping slowly by, neither of them moved.

Suddenly, M'chala spun away, his wings flapping behind him, muttering something to himself.

Jonah finally allowed himself to open his eyes again. He watched the fallen one pace around, still saying something to himself, shaking his head.

And then something dawned on him.

"You can't do it, can you? You can't hurt me," he said, finding himself almost smiling. "What, are you not allowed?"

M'chala spun violently back toward him again, screamed something unintelligible, and pulled out his own flaming red blade. Jonah had just been kidding, but he must have struck a nerve.

M'chala isn't allowed to really hurt me.

M'chala held his blade high in the air, his eyes glittering, full of rage and desire. He brought the fiery blade down hard.

Jonah held his own sword up with both hands, with just enough strength to block the fallen angel's blow. The swords pushed against each other, Jonah and M'chala clanging back and forth. M'chala was taller and stronger, though, and Jonah was slowly being shoved to the ground.

M'chala's blade was only inches away from his neck and getting closer every second. *I hope you're right about him not being able to kill you, Jonah,* he told himself. *Because if you're not . . . you're dead.*

"Jonah!" He heard the familiar voice echo down the hallway. M'chala looked up and instantly changed back into the shadowy green mist. He shot upward, only a vapor now, through an air vent in the ceiling.

Jonah turned to see Eliza leading a charge down the hall, with David at her side, bow and arrow raised. Jeremiah and Julia were close behind.

"Jonah, are you all right?" David said, immediately looking up into the vent above where M'chala had vanished. "Who was that?"

Eliza and Julia formed a shield that, together, covered all of them. "How about we discuss this in the elevator?"

Jeremiah helped pull Jonah up off the ground, and they ran down to the elevator. As they went down, they all kept a close watch on the ceiling and the crack in the door.

"How did you guys know I was here?" Jonah asked as they watched the floor numbers drop all too slowly.

"You left your Internet search up on the computer back at the convent," said Eliza. "David knew you'd left, and he came and got

Julia and me. We searched all over the convent first, and when I saw the map with the hospital pulled up . . ."

"It became clear where you were headed," finished Julia.

Jeremiah just shrugged his shoulders. "I was downstairs, trying to get into the kitchen, when I saw them wandering around, looking for you. They let me tag along."

"Well, you got to see M'chala," Jonah said as the door opened onto the second floor. "He's the fallen angel responsible for all of this." He held his arms up and pointed to the marks on his face. "Not to mention my fall yesterday."

"That was the fallen angel of all disease and sickness?" Eliza said, her mouth hanging open. David and Julia just shook their heads.

"I think so," he answered as they climbed onto the escalator. "And my guess is, he's responsible for whatever is going on with Mom too."

EIGHTEEN

A MOVING SIDEWALK

L et's just get back to the safety of the convent as fast as we can," Julia said as they hit the pavement outside. "We can sort everything out then."

They all agreed. Jonah didn't want to say it out loud, and he sensed the others didn't either. There was no telling what might be after them outside the safe walls of the convent.

"Let's move fast then," he said. He began walking so quickly with Julia and David beside him that they barely heard the screams.

"Guys! Wait!" Eliza's voice rang through the air and stopped Jonah in his tracks.

He turned to see a pair of hands sticking out of the pavement. One held Eliza's foot, the other Jeremiah's.

"What is that?" David said, his eyes growing large as they made their way back.

"Eliza and I have seen these guys before!" Jonah shouted, sprinting. "The Rephaim!"

By the time they got back to Eliza and Jeremiah, three bodies had emerged from the ground. They were not completely skeletons, but they were close. Ragged clothing hung limply on their bodies, and dirt and mold covered their faces, hands, and feet. Their faces were expressionless, with sockets for eyes.

"Help me!" Jeremiah saw his foot disappear under the concrete, and he began to panic as he tried to wrestle his arms free from the grasp of the bony arms that were pulling him.

Jonah had his sword raised as he called out to his brother.

"Jeremiah, use your belt! The belt of truth!"

But he saw movement above them too. Five fallen angels were hurtling downward beside the hospital building. M'chala had obviously sounded the alarm.

"We've got more company, guys!" Jonah called out.

While Jeremiah was busy trying to focus on the belt and not getting dragged under the earth forever, Eliza was trying to free her hands so she could raise her protective shield. But there was little she could do as she struggled against the arms of the creatures.

Julia, who had lost a few seconds staring in horror at the awful beings, snapped back into it and raised her arms above her head, forming a shield of light around all of them.

Jonah raised his angelblade and was about to strike the creature holding Eliza when he felt another hand grab at his ankle, and he lost his balance. It was so strong, it felt like it could crush the bones in his leg at any second. He caught himself on the pavement with his left hand, stood quickly, and swung with his right. The blade sliced through the wrist that was trying to pull him underground. He heard a moan come from beneath the pavement, and the hand fell to pieces around his leg.

"In the name of Elohim, go away!"

A blast of light ripped beside Jonah, and one of the Rephaim flew through the air and exploded against the corner of the building. Jeremiah had found his belt of truth and freed himself from his own attacker. He directed his next attack at the one who had Eliza.

"Elohim says that even the darkness is like light to Him!"

Another blast from his belt, and Eliza was free. She immediately raised her arms up and joined her shield with Julia's, providing a wider range of protection for them.

And just in time. The fallen angels had reached them now, spreading their wings wide to slow them down, pausing in the air just above the shields.

David's arrows were flying, but he was focusing on the attack from below. The Rephaim continued to pop up from the ground all around them, trying to wrap themselves around the quarterlings and pull them into the grave with them. David was spinning around, firing, then turning again as he saw another appear.

"Jonah!" he said as he fired again. "You have to focus on the angels!" He gave a quick nod upward. "Jeremiah and I can handle these guys!"

Jonah sheathed his sword in favor of his bow. Firing as fast as he could, he immediately hit two of the five fallen that were hovering over them. The two he hit disappeared into black dust, but the other three were attacking the shield with fury. And it seemed to be working. Eliza and Julia were straining under the pressure from above and trying to keep an eye on things at ground level.

"Jonah!" Eliza called out, letting him know that they couldn't take it much longer.

"*Jonah!*" yelled David. Four of the Rephaim had come out of the concrete at the same time. Flashes of light were coming like a lightning storm as Jeremiah spoke the words of truth as fast as he could. But they were somehow still losing ground.

Jonah continued firing at the angels above, but they were very adept at dodging arrows, and he was having a hard time aiming straight upward and finding his targets. More often than not, the flaming arrows were flying beyond them and disappearing into the darkness. He was slowing them down, but not by much.

It was time for a decision. "On my signal," Jonah called out, "run! Okay?"

He didn't wait for a response. Stringing three arrows at once, he yelled to them again, *"Now!"*

At the same time, he let the arrows fly. One of them found a target, a female fallen angel who screamed wildly as she disappeared in a cloud of black. The others had to readjust to get out of the way.

David sent one more arrow ripping through the skull of an attacker, and for a brief second, they were all free. They took their chance. Bolting ahead, they charged down the street and away from their attackers, with Jonah bringing up the rear, trying to run backward while firing as many shots as he could.

More of the Rephaim had pulled themselves out of the ground, but the quarterlings managed to put some distance between them quickly. The Rephaims' spindly legs were moving, but they weren't really getting anywhere. *I guess the dead can't really run that fast,* Jonah figured.

The fallen angels, he knew, were another matter. Jonah didn't have to look back. He felt the remaining two hot on their trail. He wondered if there were others. Or maybe M'chala himself would make another appearance.

A MOVING SIDEWALK

He saw Fifth Avenue coming up.

"Turn here!" he shouted. The kids took a right and continued running.

"There are only two left!" Eliza shouted. "We should just turn and make a stand! The Rephaim are long gone!"

Jonah knew she was right. "Okay!" he called out, nodding to David to get his arrow strung. "Ready?"

They were running down the middle of the busy avenue. They could move through people, but physical objects, like cars, buses, and taxis, were different altogether. They could get smashed if they weren't careful.

Eliza had taken the lead, though, running right down the double yellow line in the middle of the road.

Jonah looked ahead, then behind. No sign of angels—good or otherwise—in front of them, but the two behind were beginning to fire arrows. Long shots lobbed high in the air and off target, but still, they were getting closer. Now was as good a time as any to put an end to this.

Jonah began a countdown. "THREE . . . TWO . . . *ONE!*"

He dug his feet in, skidded to a stop, and turned, all in one motion. To his right, David was doing the same.

But at just the same time, the fallen angels pulled up. They rose in the air, turned around, and flew backward, retreating into the darkness.

"They're scared!" said Jeremiah. "They know they aren't any match for us, so they're running."

He gave David a high five, laughing in the middle of the busy street, cars still whizzing by.

Jonah felt his back stiffen as he watched the two black-winged demons disappear.

"So what did you say those things were?" David asked. "The Rephaim?"

"It means 'dead ones' in Hebrew. And that's pretty much what they are," Eliza said. "Somehow Abaddon has control of them."

As David and Eliza discussed this, other questions began to nibble around the edge of Jonah's brain.

Why haven't more fallen angels come after us too? And why would those just give up the chase?

"Let's go," he muttered, cutting their celebration short.

NINETEEN

THE THING BEYOND
THE MIST

They moved over to the sidewalk, sidestepping a couple of screeching taxicabs along the way. Eliza wasn't celebrating anymore either. Jonah saw her thoughts churning, probably just like his.

"That whole thing was weird," she finally said as they sped along beside the relative safety of the expensive shops on Fifth Avenue. "Strange, huh, Jonah?"

"What do you mean?" asked Julia. "We ran them off. Right?" The question was asked with a total lack of confidence.

"Right, Jonah?" she said again.

Jonah shrugged. "I just keep asking myself—why would they just leave? I mean . . . they never do that. They stay until the end. It's not in their nature to run away."

David was looking ahead, at the next block up. It was normally one of those places where the bright lights of the city would be blinding, glittering with advertisements and enticements to enter and buy.

But now, it somehow looked murkier. Darker.

"Guys, look at this . . . ," he said.

Jeremiah studied it. "Why is it so dark up there?"

"Hold on a second, guys," Eliza said. "Let me check this out."

In a flash, she had left the hidden realm. They could still see her, but she was unable to see them. Knowing they were there, she spoke aloud. "It's bright out here, no sign of any darkness. It's all happening in the hidden realm."

She bowed to pray and was back with them in an instant.

Whatever the darkness was, it was moving like a slow thunderstorm in their direction. The closer the cloud came, the more Jonah sensed the presence of cold evil.

"Do you hear that?" asked David, looking with his mouth wide open over at Jonah and the others. Everyone nodded.

There was a snorting noise coming from the cloud, and it was getting louder.

"It sounds like when we went to the zoo that time," said Jeremiah. Jonah looked at him blankly. "You know, the rhino section?"

Jonah was still trying to make the connection when it was made for him. The sharp protrusion of some kind of horn emerged from the cloud, as tall as a ten-story building, right in front of them. It was attached to the largest snout that Jonah had ever seen, covered in gray, black, and green scales. There were three horns, on top of the snout with razor-sharp tips, pointing toward the heavens.

The face of the creature came into view, even more awful than the sight of the horns alone. Its head was bigger than the cargo van that sat outside the store.

"A stegosaurus?" Jeremiah said wildly, in a high-pitched tone. "There are dinosaurs here?"

Jonah shook his head. It didn't have the hood of armor around its head like that old dinosaur, but it sure did look more like a dinosaur than anything he had ever seen. It stepped its giant foot forward, crashing into the pavement. Raising its head, it snorted, dark smoke billowing from its nose.

"I guess we know why the street is getting so dark," said Eliza.

It stepped with its other front foot, drawing closer to them. Its body was becoming visible now, and Jonah couldn't help but be in awe. It had a massive trunk, made of the same scaly skin that looked thicker than the shell of a tank. Four powerful legs propelled it forward, its muscles rippling through them as it moved.

Something moved behind it, the clouds separating as though being blown away.

"Is there another one?" asked David.

Jonah stared closely at the wavering cloud. "No, I think it's . . . its tail."

The giant beast took another step forward and proved Jonah right. It had the largest tail he had ever seen on any animal, seemingly double the length of its body. It was swaying back and forth, and on the end was a large ball with spikes all over it, just like the three covering its head.

The worst thing of all, though, was that it appeared to be looking right at them.

"I think we know why the fallen angels were scared off," Jonah called out. "It wasn't because of us!"

The creature raised its head and issued a deafening roar.

"And I don't think it's very happy!" said David.

Eliza studied the creature. "It's being controlled by Abaddon.

Just like the rest of the creatures we've encountered along the way. Just like the leviathan."

"Any ideas, Jonah?" David asked, his voice starting to waver. Jonah knew that if his brave Ugandan friend was getting scared, they were truly in trouble.

But then Jeremiah took three large steps forward and stood on the street corner, in plain view of the creature. Jonah could see his legs shaking, but his belt of truth appeared.

"We all know that the strength of Elohim is greater than Abaddon's, or yours, or anyone else's!" he shouted. "So just go back to where you came from!"

His belt flashed a brilliant light, erupting upward and into the creature's face. A white explosion collided with the darkness, and for a minute, the giant disappeared from view.

"Nice one, Jeremiah!" Eliza said. But then she started scolding. "Now get back over here beside me before something else happens!" Jeremiah obediently stepped back toward her, with all eyes still on the creature above.

"I guess that takes care of it," he said, slapping the dirt off his hands.

An even louder roar erupted, though, letting them know this battle was far from over. The blast of the creature's breath blew the clouds back. It was there, searching for the kids again, and when it spotted them, it glared as if even more annoyed.

"It was blinded for a second," Jonah said. "But looks like it's going to take more than that to defeat it."

Jonah took a deep breath and pulled out his bow. He stood out on the street, in front of the creature, and began firing, over and over again. David did the same. Each time, their arrows were true, striking the monster in the face and the chest.

But the flaming arrows kept bouncing off, falling harmlessly onto the ground.

"It's got some kind of armor," Jonah said. "These arrows are not going to do the trick."

"But I do think we've made it angry!" shouted David.

The creature began slamming its tail on the ground. *Wham! Wham! Wham!* It felt like the road was going to split in half every time its giant tail crashed into the pavement. The ground underneath the quarterlings shook, and all the while, cars in the physical world were still driving by as if nothing were going on, and people strolled down the street, completely unaware of the hidden realm.

"I need to look up something!" Eliza suddenly said.

Jonah's eyes were trained on the monster, but he shot his sister a harsh look. "This is no time for school research, Eliza!"

"No, just trust me," she called out. "I need to find out something... Distract it for a few minutes. David, hand me your Bible!"

David dug into the back pocket of his jeans and produced a small Bible he liked to carry. He tossed it to her, and she crouched down underneath an awning, out of view of the creature, and began to thumb through the pages.

Distract it? How am I supposed to do that and not get eaten? Jonah's mind raced. All the while, the monster was getting closer. It seemed to have narrowed its focus on Jonah. After all, he was the one shooting all the arrows at it.

Jonah ran to the other side of the street, narrowly avoiding getting hit by a city bus.

"Hey, ugly!" he shouted, waving his arms in the air and jumping up and down. "I'm over here! You think you can catch me? I think you're too big and slow!"

The creature did, indeed, have its attention on him. It turned toward him, leaning its head down and growling low.

"It's working, Jonah!" David called out from the other side of the street.

"Great," Jonah answered. "Glad I could help out." *Just great. Now all it wants to do is have me for a late-night snack. Glad I could help you out so you could do a little more studying, Eliza.*

Jonah stopped waving his arms as he found himself stepping backward, and the beast grew closer. He felt a brick wall behind him and knew he was almost trapped.

"I hope you figure out something soon, Eliza!" he yelled across the street.

She held up a finger in the air as she studied. "Just one more minute!"

"I don't have one more minute!" Jonah called out. "In ten seconds, I might be headed down the throat of this thing!"

The creature lowered its head, pointing its horns directly at him. One of its enormous front legs began pawing at the ground. It snorted loudly again.

"That thing's going to rush Jonah!" said Julia.

David, Jeremiah, and Julia bolted across the street with Jonah, screaming and waving as loudly as they could.

"Hey, over here, over here!"

"Look at us!"

Julia had produced the shield of faith above her head and was trying to use it to get the beast's attention. Jeremiah continued with the belt of truth, even though he knew it wasn't going to work. At least maybe it would confuse the thing. David began firing arrows in between Jonah and the creature, trying to draw its attention away again.

The creature turned its head toward the three, as if considering going after them instead. But then it lowered its head again and charged.

If Jonah hadn't possessed angelic superstrength, he would never have survived the bull-rush attack. But he sprang out of the way just as its giant, scaly head connected hard with the side of the building.

"Way too close, guys!" he shouted as he landed on his shoulder hard on the cement.

The giant turned toward him and then back to the others, as if it were deciding whom to go after next. Just then, a metal side door to the building opened, and a short man emerged, carrying two bags of trash to the sidewalk. Jonah saw his chance. He jumped up and dove through the door, just after the horn from the beast's head crashed behind him. Thankfully, its head was too large to fit through the opening.

Jonah found himself on the floor of a jewelry store. As he was picking himself up off the ground, David, Jeremiah, and Julia slid through the doorway, just in front of the short man, who closed the door behind him and turned the lock.

"You guys all right?" Jonah asked, picking himself up. They nodded, turning toward the windows of the corner store. A giant green eyeball appeared, and as it spotted them in the store, it narrowed into a slit.

Then it opened again. Jonah felt even queasier. The creature picked its head up and turned around. *What's it doing?*

"It's going after Eliza," said Julia. They ran to the front double doors of the store. She was standing on the opposite street corner, the Bible open in one hand, its pages fluttering in the breeze. Her mouth was open as she stared upward at the monster.

It had apparently decided that its best chance for a meal would be her.

Jonah pressed his face against the windowpane, beating on the glass. "Eliza! Come on!" He beckoned with his hands for her to run over.

She had seen them enter the building and looked across at them now, keeping one eye on the approaching monster. She was pointing to the Bible and then up at the beast. Then she made a waving motion with her hand.

"What's she doing?" asked Julia, looking at Eliza curiously.

"Looks like she is pretending to hold a sword," answered Jeremiah.

"And it looks like she's found something in the Scriptures about this creature," said David.

Jonah was already working on unlatching the locked front door. He didn't know what this thing was, but he knew what Eliza needed him to do. She continued to point to the Bible and make sword motions, but the creature was advancing on her now. Jonah heard her piercing scream and lost her behind the enormous body of the beast.

Its giant tail was like a massive telephone pole, swinging randomly back and forth.

"I'm coming, Eliza! Hang on!" he called out as he tried to navigate the tail. "Use your shield!"

He couldn't tell what was going on, or if she even heard him, though. He could only utter a quick prayer and try to get to her before anything bad happened.

Elohim, protect her.

The tail swung back toward him, and he ducked. As soon as it passed, he knew he had about one full second. It was enough.

He ran and jumped, unsheathing his sword at the same time. Even though the scales on the back of the giant looked rough, he found them to be slick, almost glass-like. He slipped as soon as he landed just above the creature's back legs. Standing again, he wobbled, as if he were trying to run along the curve of a giant glass bottle someone was shaking.

Thankfully, the creature must not have noticed him, so intent on its pursuit of Eliza now. *If I can just get to its head . . .*

Jonah was halfway up its back when he heard Eliza scream again. It was a different kind of sound—louder, deeper—and he knew that he had only a couple of seconds before she would be gone.

He felt something deep inside him well up—his love for his sister, along with an anger that this beast would dare attack any of them, especially her—and he grabbed his angelblade hilt with both hands. Taking two more steps, he leaped toward the beast's head.

But just as he did, the creature reared back its head, and Jonah flew off, slamming into the city street below. His blade clattered away.

"Eliza!"

The monster dove its head toward Eliza, and all he could do was watch.

But just then, its jaws spun away and it let out a loud sound, more a gurgling noise than a roar. Jonah rolled out of the way just as the powerful beast toppled over on its side. The force of the fall shook the earth beneath them.

He stood up, unable to see around the beast. Frantically, he worked his way around, calling out Eliza's name, expecting the worst. Anticipating the sight of her limp body on the concrete sidewalk.

"Eliza!"

But she was standing beside a hot dog cart with one arm raised. And in that hand, the one that had held the Bible, was something else.

An angelblade.

TWENTY

ANOTHER TEST

Jonah shouted to her and ran to her side. Eliza blinked a few times, looking upward at the sword, then over to the beast lying still in the middle of the road, vehicles cruising through it, unaware.

David, Julia, and Jeremiah came running across the street.

"Wow, Eliza," said Jeremiah. "That is so cool! Where did you get it?" He marveled at the sword as she held it in front of her.

"The Bible I was holding . . . ," she said, stumbling over her words. "That Bible . . . it turned into this sword."

It was fiery and a bright shade of green, almost neon. The blade was a little smaller than Jonah's. She waved it in front of her slowly.

"It's so light," she said.

Jonah smiled. "They're made to fit their owners perfectly, you know. It's made for you, and only you."

She blinked a couple of times, then sheathed it beside her hip. It disappeared.

"We have to go," she said, pulling them along with her around the behemoth and across the street. "And I mean *now.*"

"What is the rush, Eliza?" asked Julia. "I don't see any other creatures out here."

Eliza looked back at the creature, lying still on the road. "It's just what I thought. A behemoth."

"It's gone, Eliza," Jonah said, trying to comfort her. "You got it." He could feel her frayed nerves himself. She shook her head a few times, as if she didn't believe him.

"I don't think so. I think I just stunned it," she said. "I remembered this creature was spoken of, along with the leviathan, in the book of Job. Two of the most powerful creatures Elohim ever created. The verse said something really specific." She closed her eyes, recalling it word for word.

"Its tail sways like a cedar; the sinews of its thighs are close-knit. Its bones are tubes of bronze, its limbs like rods of iron. It ranks first among the works of God, yet its Maker can approach it with his sword."

Jonah glanced over at David. "See there, Eliza? It says it can be defeated with a sword. That's what you did, right?"

She was still shaking her head, though. "No, we need to get out of here now. That's not what it means. Whose sword does it talk about?"

She was watching the behemoth as she waited for his answer.

"Its Maker's," said Jonah softly. He looked back over at the behemoth. "But he's not . . ." Just then the creature started to twitch. "Moving."

But he *was* moving, and no sooner had Jonah spoken those words than the beast shook violently and crouched up on its front feet.

"Run!" Jonah and David said it at the same time, not that the others needed to be told.

Jonah scanned for an escape route as they bolted across the street and past the jewelry store. The behemoth was up and very, very angry. He could hear the rumbling steps behind him and chose not to look backward.

"The subway!" he shouted, pointing to the downward staircase on the other side of the street.

"Again?" Jeremiah moaned, but they had no choice. The monster wouldn't be able to make it down the steps.

They bounded underneath the ground just as the behemoth got to the edge of the steps. All it could do was roar loudly as the quarterlings disappeared around the corner.

The short subway ride home was quiet. They all cut their eyes back and forth around the car. Jonah couldn't remember what it felt like not to be at least a little paranoid wherever he went. With the happenings of the last hour, though, his jumpiness had gone into overdrive.

"The Bible says the behemoth can be controlled only by the sword of Elohim," Eliza finally said quietly. They had come out of the hidden realm and were back among the visible, with regular people sitting all around.

Jonah's head pounded harder than ever before, so much that he began to feel dizzy. He looked at her with half-open eyes. "How was I supposed to know what you were saying from inside a store and all the way across the street?" His voice had risen louder than he wanted, earning him stares from a couple of the people sitting nearby. When he stared back, they quickly looked away. *It's pretty bad when you catch looks from crazy subway people,* he thought to himself.

Eliza threw her hands up. "I just think that you shouldn't always be so rash. One of these days you're going to really get yourself hurt . . . or worse," she said. She had always been unwilling to back down from Jonah, and now was no different.

Julia sighed. "I have to agree with her, Jonah. You've put us all in danger again. How many times is that now?"

Jonah boiled over. "Nobody told you to follow me! I didn't ask you to come to the hospital! And how was I supposed to know we'd be attacked on the streets by that monster?"

David looked at him sincerely. "Because that's what always happens when we're with you, Jonah."

Jeremiah spoke up. "I thought it was pretty awesome to fight the behemoth," he said quietly.

At least Jeremiah's not throwing me under the bus, Jonah thought.

"You could have been killed too, Jeremiah," Eliza said.

Jonah caught the sound of dark whispering again, but he was growing so angry he ignored it, his voice rising almost to a shout. "I suppose I should have let the behemoth have you then!" The whole back half of the car turned, but he didn't care.

"Jonah!" Julia whispered loudly, trying not to make eye contact with the people who were suddenly watching them. She motioned toward them with her head.

"I was trying to do the right thing. I wanted to find M'chala. I just thought that I could do something about all of this. Stop anyone else from getting hurt. I think I'm the one he wants."

"You did find M'chala," observed Jeremiah. "And that guy was creepy. Way worse than any fallen angels I've seen."

Jonah put his hand on the back of Jeremiah's neck. Once again, he had rushed into things without a fully formed plan. This make-it-up-as-you-go attitude was going to catch up with him eventually. And now everyone was mad at him again.

They switched trains so they would land as close to the convent as possible. They planned on making a run for it, just in case they had been identified and were being tracked by the fallen angels, or worse, the apparently undefeatable behemoth.

In the darkness, they entered back into the hidden realm and then jogged three blocks back home. Their eyes were everywhere—in front of them, behind, and upward. Jonah saw the angels, standing ever vigilant around the building above. *Would have been nice to have a few of them with us back there,* he thought. He caught the glare of several of them, no doubt wondering where this group of kids had been.

It was already the wee hours of the morning. They made immediate beelines for their rooms, agreeing that they all needed sleep before regrouping the next morning.

"Are you ready for competition tomorrow?" Jeremiah asked, half-asleep as he walked up the stairs.

Jonah didn't feel ready for anything except sleep. His body ached, his head still throbbed, and the sores all over his body itched. He couldn't get comfortable. He tried to rub his arm, but when he touched the sensitive spots, which were everywhere, he almost cried. One name kept coming to mind over and over again. The one reason he had this affliction. And, he had become convinced, the reason he'd had the dizzy spell in the tree.

His mouth hardened as he whispered the name.

"M'chala."

Jonah awoke in a sweat, but it wasn't the picture of the monster behemoth breathing down his neck on his mind. The image of the green shadow of the fallen angel that had appeared out of the ceiling at the hospital dominated his thoughts. He was sure he had dreamed about him, although he couldn't remember any details. It was that feeling that he disliked. It reminded him of the iciest of days deep in the winter in Peacefield, when dark clouds rolled in from the west—cold and full of dread.

Where was that evil creature? Where was he going to show his ugly face next? Whom would he harm? Those questions relentlessly pounded inside him, and he couldn't seem to shake them free.

He lay in bed, unable to go back to sleep and unwilling to get up yet. He could tell his back was going to hurt all day. His body ached. All of it was finally catching up with him. Hot tears burned in his eyes, and he muffled his face in his pillow so David wouldn't hear him cry. His chest heaved in silence as he let out all of his frustration and heaviness, pressing the pillow even tighter onto his face.

"Elohim," he whispered as his chest finally slowed. "I don't know what to do. I don't know what is going on. All I know is that I feel awful, and responsible, and like this all has something to do with me. I haven't meant to, but I'm bringing my friends into this. They're suffering because of me. David and Julia, they almost died because of me. And Eliza . . ." He paused as the emotions welled up again, crashing over him like yet another ocean wave.

He continued his conversation with Elohim. "I want to believe that all of this is in Your plan. I want to be able to trust You. I know that's what my dad would say to do right now. I just feel so lost."

Jonah listened to himself breathe for a while, and gradually the exhalations grew further and further apart, and steadier. He had poured out his doubts to Elohim. He had seen Elohim work before, and his whole life was all the evidence he needed that He was real.

The words that he spoke next felt more like they had come from somewhere else than him.

"Whatever You do is okay," he whispered. "Whatever happens, I'm here. I put myself totally in Your hands today."

The next wave that came over him was a strange, exhilarating feeling, the kind he got when he saw his mom and dad watching him play basketball. Someone delighted in him. It had to be Elohim.

With new strength, Jonah pushed himself out of bed and headed for the showers. In spite of everything, he found himself getting excited about today's exam. It would be a full-fledged battle simulation that would challenge all of their abilities, and then some. But as he exited the bathroom, there was one thing he wanted to do first.

⌒⌒

Taryn stood with him outside of the convent and once again raised her hands to create an Angelic Vortex.

"Thanks for letting me speak to my parents," Jonah said as they stood in the middle. He needed to check on his mom. Especially after discovering that it was likely M'chala who was responsible not only for his troubles, but for hers as well.

The image of his father's face came up on the screen, along with an angel standing beside him.

"Son," Benjamin said, rubbing his eyes beneath his glasses.

"This is a nice surprise. It's good to see you this morning." He leaned forward, looking Jonah up and down. "Doesn't look like you are doing any better, though. Actually, you look worse."

"Yeah," Jonah said. "My head is still hurting, and the sores are awful. But I didn't really get in touch to talk about that. I was wondering how Mom is. Where is she? Is she okay?" Not seeing her there worried him.

"She's still in bed," responded Benjamin. He sighed loudly, as if he were letting his guard down for the first time in a while. "She's not doing very well, to tell you the truth. The doctors are stumped. She just keeps getting weaker. I told her you wanted to talk, but she couldn't get herself up."

"Well, here I am," came a weakened voice. Jonah watched his mom push herself through the vortex and come into view on the screen. Her hair was pulled back off her face, which looked tired and creased. She looked thinner than Jonah had ever seen her. "Hi, Jonah," she said, forcing a smile.

"Mom . . ." Jonah never wanted to give her a hug as much as he did right then. "Dad was just telling me that they don't know what's going on with you."

She rested her head softly on Benjamin's shoulder, closing her eyes for a few seconds. "I'm sure the doctors will be able to figure me out. You don't need to worry about a thing. You have a big exam today, I hear."

Jonah shook his head. "I don't care about that, Mom. I had an encounter last night, one that made me realize that the things I am going through and your sickness are probably connected."

Benjamin perked up. "What do you mean?"

He told them about discovering M'chala and his confrontation in the hospital. "For some reason, he's been tormenting me with these sores and making me feel awful. But I think he's also been responsible for people around me getting hurt."

Benjamin eyed Eleanor, placing his arm around her shoulder. "We have suspected that there might be something like that going on here. We've been praying for her protection and healing every day."

What else could they do? Jonah was at a loss. "Just keep fighting, Mom," he said. "Keep fighting. Promise me that you will, okay?"

She nodded. "We're going to get through this, Jonah. I'll be okay. Please don't worry about me. This is a big day for you."

They said their good-byes, and Jonah walked slowly back into the convent.

He saw the quarterlings enter the meal hall, jabbering about the upcoming day's big event. Nervous, loud laughter was coming from the room, but Jonah suddenly wasn't in the mood to join them.

Passing by the room, he shuffled down the hall farther, unable to get his mother off his mind. He found himself in front of Camilla's office door, which was cracked open. Peeking through the slit in the door, he saw a winged figure in a glittering blue garment facing the window, standing perfectly still.

He pushed the door open and waited.

"Jonah," Camilla said without looking back. "Are you okay?"

Jonah stepped into her office and slumped down in one of the chairs in front of her desk. *Am I okay? I am not even sure how to answer that question.*

He shrugged his shoulders. "Something happened last night."

"I know," she said, turning toward him now. "I spoke with Eliza this morning."

It hit him that he had never seen her look more tired. The

lines on her face were somehow deeper and more pronounced. She reminded him more in this moment of the Camilla Aldridge of his past, the feeble woman who sometimes walked with a cane down the aisle of their old church in Peacefield.

"Then you heard about M'chala," he said. "I found him. I tried to . . . I wanted to . . . I don't know. Stop him, I guess. But I couldn't. And now . . ."

She nodded, raising an eyebrow. "Yes, Jonah?"

"And now he's attacked my mother, and there isn't a thing I can do about it!" he blurted out, grabbing onto the armrests of the chair.

Camilla moved around, sitting on the edge of her desk, right in front of him. She looked down at him with love and compassion. "There are many things in life that we cannot control, Jonah."

He slammed his fist down on the chair arm, snapping the wood in two. "Sorry," he said, holding a piece of broken wood in his hands, "but that's not really what I want to hear right now."

She nodded, ignoring the broken chair. "It never is."

Jonah and Camilla sat in the room in silence for a few minutes. Finally, Jonah peered up at her again.

"I just want to know what's going on."

"You are being tested, Jonah. There is no doubt about that." She sighed and seemed as if she were about to tell him something more, then thought better of it. "Your decision, in the midst of all the uncertainty and pain, is how you are going to respond. What will you do when pushed to your limit, and then beyond? Will you turn toward Elohim with everything you have, or turn away? That is all in this life you really can determine anyway."

"That's it?" Jonah didn't like hearing that things were out of his control. That there was nothing he could do to fix his problems. He also knew, though, that as much as he didn't like it, those words were true.

Camilla moved back around to her window again without a word, and Jonah knew this was her signal that the conversation was over. He stood and made his way to the dining hall.

❧

An hour later, all the quarterlings were gathered in the lobby of the convent, waiting for the messenger angels to appear, along with Camilla. The quarterlings were standing in small groups, filling the hall with nervous chatter as they took turns offering opinions on what the final exams would look like today. Jonah stood quietly to the side, hands shoved down in his pockets, glancing at the other kids every so often but mainly staring down blankly at the wooden floor.

"Hey," a voice came from behind. He turned to find Eliza walking up behind him and attempting to smile.

"Hey, Eliza," he said.

"You look like you have a lot on your mind," she offered. He knew it was her way of breaking the ice, letting him know she wasn't mad at him anymore. He felt his shoulders relax a little, and he exhaled softly.

"Yeah, I guess I do," he said, and proceeded to tell her about his conversation with their parents in the Angelic Vortex a little while ago. "Mom didn't look very good at all," he said, unwilling to sugarcoat it. And then he blurted out, "And I'm sorry, Eliza, about putting you all in so much danger. I—"

"I know," she interrupted. Then she did something very un-Eliza-like. Wrapping her arms around his shoulders, she hugged him tightly. "I forgive you. And mainly, you've just been trying to do the right thing. It just hasn't worked out all that well."

Jonah smiled at his sister. "Yet," he said, causing her to roll her eyes.

"I'm worried about Mom," she finally said, still holding him tightly. He didn't know what to say but didn't push her away.

She stepped away from him and patted him on the shoulder. "Well, just do me a favor and don't get yourself hurt anymore out there today, okay?"

Precisely at ten o'clock, Camilla and the messenger angels appeared with a flash.

"Today is your final exam, and it will play out a little differently than the others," Camilla said. "As you know, these exams are to test your skills as quarterlings. It is not to be seen as a contest to create rivalry among you." As she said this, she glared at Jonah, and then Frederick. "That said, today's contest involves everyone. It will demand that you utilize all of your abilities. What is more, you will be called upon to rely on Elohim. Yes, your trust in Him will be tested, challenged, and stretched. Now, if we don't leave immediately, we are going to be late. Shall we?"

When Jonah landed, he found himself on the outcropping of a mountain, sitting high over a beach lapped by clear blue water. A few sailboats traveled lazily in the distance. The warmth of the sun felt good, and the cool breeze blowing against his face even better.

He looked around and realized he was entirely alone.

TWENTY-ONE

THE FINAL STAGE

W ow," Jonah said as he took a few minutes to check out his new surroundings and get adjusted. It wasn't simply a mountain he was on, but a ridge that curved around and around far off in the distance, and all the way back to him again. The ridge formed a circle, which looked almost perfectly round. He had been on top of mountains before, but never one quite like this.

On the outer edge of the mountain, the rugged, rocky terrain at the top gradually gave way to lush green vegetation, and then a sandy beach. Crystal blue waves lapped against it.

The interior of the circled ridge was similar. A steep, rocky hill going down, in some places almost vertical, connecting with low-lying brush, and then thicker green vegetation, like a rain forest.

"Welcome to Hawaii!" a booming voice called out, though Jonah couldn't see him. It was Nathaniel. "We're standing on the edge of a crater formed by a volcano long ago. Gorgeous, isn't it?"

A crater, Jonah thought. That was why the ridge formed a

perfect circle. He looked closely now, along the highest point of the crater that was even with him. He could make out people spaced out along the edge all the way around. They were each about the same distance from one another.

So that's where everyone else ended up. Camilla was right. We're all going to compete against one another this time.

His eyes were suddenly drawn upward as a platform materialized above him, like the one he'd seen in the first competition. Glancing to his right and left, he saw that there were other platforms in the distance, forming in front of the other quarterlings.

A giant head appeared in front of him. Jonah couldn't help but think it looked like a head on a platter. It belonged to Nathaniel.

"It's a beautiful setting, isn't it, friends? We decided you deserved your own special venue for this final test: the battle simulation. We're on a stunning crater on an equally gorgeous Hawaiian island. But don't let the scenery fool you," he said. His giant eyes looked down toward the crater's center. "In between here and there, a whole host of challenges awaits you. In this final part of your examinations, as you likely have noticed, you will all be competing against one another. Every skill you have will be tested. Each of you possesses unique skills, and the ability lies within you to complete this task. Even the smallest of you have an equal chance, based on the course laid out in front of you."

Jonah looked down in front of him but saw no course laid out. No track to follow. Just rocks, and then a lush forest beyond.

"Look carefully now at the center of the rain forest below," Nathaniel said. As he said this, a flag was being raised, higher and higher, so that it came into full view. It was enormous, with every stripe of a rainbow on it, and in the middle, a set of white angel wings. "The flag that is being raised is your destination. The goal is simple—get to that flag as fast as you can. Any way you can. There will be obstacles in your way, specifically designed with you in mind. They are to test your strength, courage, perseverance, and faith in Elohim. I cannot tell you what you are about to face. What I can say is that the challenge will be just as difficult spiritually and mentally as it will be physically."

The smile had drained from Nathaniel's face now, and he looked entirely serious.

"Now, according to your test scores so far, Frederick is at the top of your class, followed by Eliza and Jonah. But this is your biggest test, and it carries the most weight. Do well, and any one of you could steal the top spot!"

This should be piece of cake compared to that behemoth last night, Jonah thought, looking down the mountainside and plotting the best route to take to get to the forest and then to the flag. He knew, though, that it wouldn't be as easy as running down a hill and through the woods. His heart rate began to quicken as he thought about the prospect of facing the unknown obstacles that Nathaniel spoke of.

"And one more thing," Nathaniel's voice boomed again. "Today, a special surprise. You each have visitors here to cheer you on."

Jonah heard the cheers before he saw their images appear on the platform. A picture materialized of a group of people seated on a small set of bleachers around the flag. A close-up of his parents flashed in front of him, and he imagined that Eliza and Jeremiah were seeing the same image. His dad waved wildly and smiled at them.

"Mom!" he said, even though he knew she couldn't hear him.

She had made it and was waving, but looked weak and pale. She managed a smile, but it appeared to take a lot of effort even for that. He was reminded again how sick she looked, but he tried to force that out of his mind for the time being.

After the image of his parents, a quick shot of each of the quarterlings popped into view. When they came up, each one waved, gave a thumbs-up, or nodded at the screen. When it was Jonah's turn, he gave a small wave of his hand.

"Okay, quarterlings," Nathaniel said, his head reappearing. "On your mark, get set . . ." Jonah wondered if his parents would be able to watch him on a screen of their own.

"Go!"

The platform, along with Nathaniel's head, disappeared. Jonah looked at the flag again, getting his bearings, and then began down the steep embankment in front of him.

The slope was so severe in some places that he had to zigzag to make his way down safely. Back and forth, back and forth. He came to a place with a face of sheer rock, straight down for at least twenty feet.

"Angel strength, I hope you're still with me," he said and lowered himself, face forward, down onto the rock. His fingers found a crack in the rock, and his feet were pressed into two dimples.

He took a deep breath and began his descent down the cliff face slowly.

"Just one finger hold at a time, Jonah," he muttered to himself.

His fingers found another crack, and he lowered himself down again. Six inches at a time, he made his way down the rock face, all along wondering if he was moving too slowly and who might be ahead of him now. In his mind, anyway, Frederick was already ahead of him.

As Jonah distracted himself with this thought, his feet slipped, and he found himself dangling over a group of craggy rocks below with two fingers from each hand stuffed into cracks. His feet frantically searched for holds along the rock as his fingers quickly grew weaker. Even his angel strength had limits, and this was certainly going to test them.

He gathered himself and pulled his right hand out so that for the briefest second he was holding himself up by two fingers alone. Quickly, though, he found another handhold farther down, pulling his other hand out. He found rest for one of his feet and took a few seconds to catch his breath.

Jonah navigated the rest of the face without too much trouble, and soon found himself working his way around the craggy rocks on the floor of the crater.

A stretch of rough but relatively flat terrain opened up in front of him, about the length of a football field between him and the beginning of the rain forest. He guessed it was double that from there to the flagpole. And he was determined to be the first quarterling to arrive.

Jonah was about to call on his winged feet to sprint ahead, when a shadow passed over him. Then another and another. He looked up to see at least half a dozen angels—disguised as the Fallen, of course—diving toward him. He didn't panic. He'd been in this situation before, and he reminded himself that they weren't real.

Finding his arrows, he crouched down behind a rock and began firing. He connected with the closest two attackers. Another angel fired at him, and he leaned back just in time to watch the arrow blast into the sand.

That was close, he said to himself as he knelt behind the rock, his back toward the approaching angels. With another arrow in his hand, he turned in one motion, locked in on the nearest angel, and released. The arrow was true to its mark.

Easy as a LeBron James fast-break dunk.

The remaining two angels soared upward, out of range. He glanced toward the forest and decided his best bet was to make a break for the trees. Summoning his sandals of speed, he bolted in that direction.

Halfway there, he felt a sudden stinging sensation in his shoulder.

"Ow!" he said, hitting the ground as he clutched at his arm. The way it felt, he expected to see an arrow sticking all the way through his shoulder. But there was nothing there. It only felt as if there were.

He held his shoulder and stood back up, continuing to run, but looking backward at the pursuing angels. One of them was poised to fire again, and he bore down toward the trees, hunching his back down.

"Agh!" Again, a similar pain shot through his right leg, the arrow connecting with the back of his knee. He dropped to the ground and instinctively held his leg. Drawing his hand back, though, he saw there was no blood. His jeans weren't even ripped. He only felt the pain of the arrow, not the arrow itself.

"It's not there, Jonah," he repeated to himself over and over. "It's not there; it's just in your head. The pain's not real." But it sure felt real.

The angels made a dive at him, missed, and moved beyond, climbing back up. They would definitely be back for another pass. Jonah forced himself off the ground and half limped, half ran toward the trees once again.

He knew they were turning above him in the sky, but he stayed focused on the green brush just ahead. When he was almost there, he visualized another arrow piercing him in the back, and he dove as hard as he could. Falling into a patch of thick grass that covered his head and the rest of him, he felt an arrow whiz past his ear and hit the ground just ahead.

Army-crawling forward, he pulled himself toward the trees and into the brush, suddenly thick around him. There was a canopy above, and he assumed that, unless the angels pursued him, he was safe for the time being.

Jonah stood up, working the pain out of his knee by pressing his hands on it for a few seconds. He did the same on his shoulder, which seemed to help a little. But he also knew that part of this challenge, like Nathaniel said, was about dealing with physical pain. The image of Frederick running athletically toward the flag played across the screen in his mind again, and he pushed the pain away.

"Hopefully he has his own set of fallen angels to deal with over there," he muttered.

Jonah hurried through the brush and trees, and at first, he felt as if he were making good time. But it was growing thicker with every step, until it was like a series of heavy curtains that he found himself pushing back and stepping through. All around him was the brush of this jungle, and he was beginning to feel a little claustrophobic.

Turning around, he realized he was closed in on every side. He spun around to try to figure out where he was, but immediately wished he hadn't. Because now he was questioning which way he had been headed in the first place.

"Which way is the flagpole?" He mumbled the question, realizing that every direction looked the same. Making his best guess, he moved forward, pressing his body against the thick grass, forcing the thought out of his mind that he may be going the wrong way.

SHADOW CHASER

Jonah had also begun to lose track of time. The more he pushed himself though, the more he felt like hours were passing by. It was light, but only barely, the sun unable to break through the thick trees above. Sweat rolled down his cheeks, and he periodically wiped his face on his sleeve. Had it been five minutes? Thirty? Two hours? He was losing track of things, and with each step and no sign of the end of the jungle, something dark and lonely increased its grip on him.

Just when he thought he couldn't move another foot forward, the brush in front of him began to grow lighter. He took a few more steps, and it was thinner still, until suddenly, he spilled out into a clearing.

It was brighter here, the sun peeking through a little more, and the ground was damp and covered with all kinds of plants and grasses. Just ahead, he heard the sound of falling water. He moved forward, toward a low waterfall pouring into a pool. It extended into a creek winding through the rain forest.

Jonah stopped quickly, realizing there was someone with his back turned to him, crouching down in front of the pool. The person didn't seem to notice him, or at least pretended not to. There were no wings on his back, but Jonah felt his heart rate quicken, and he pulled his angelblade out as he approached.

"You aren't going to use that on me, are you?" the man said without turning around. "Come look at these fish. They really are amazing."

Jonah recognized his voice before he saw his face. "You again?"

He moved up beside the man he had walked with on the beach, the one who had been surfing. He felt his own arm, remembering the feelings of peace that had washed over him when the man touched him.

The man turned, greeting Jonah with a smile. Jonah looked down into the pool, teeming with large fish, orange, white, and black. "Koi?"

"Gorgeous, aren't they?" the man said, holding his hand down. The fish swarmed around his hand, which just touched the water. He was feeding them something.

Jonah pointed his thumb over his shoulder. "I . . . uh . . . have to get going. But you know that, right?"

He stood up now, beside Jonah. "Don't worry," he said, his clear eyes studying him. "You're not losing any time in the race right now."

"What's that supposed to mean?"

"Let's just say that time works a little differently in this part of the competition," the man said. "But I won't keep you long. I just want to remind you of what I said a while back."

Jonah eyed him. "Back on the beach?"

"Yeah," the man said, throwing his remaining handful of food to the fish, which almost jumped out of the water to get it. "You remember, right?"

Jonah thought for a second. "You said that I need to be prepared for anything. I think your words were that 'dark days are coming,' and that I need to remember to trust Elohim no matter what."

He nodded at Jonah, the smile fading just a little. "Yes," he said. "Good. I'm glad you didn't forget our conversation. There are some things that are going to happen, and happen soon, that will test you in some ways that you haven't been tested before. Some things you are afraid of."

"What's going to happen?" Jonah asked. "You can tell me, can't you? I would be better prepared if I knew."

He smiled again, patting him on the shoulder. Jonah winced when he touched his shoulder, but realized that it no longer hurt from the arrow shot. Nor did his knee. "There are some things that Elohim will reveal only when He wants to. If they haven't been shown to you, then in His best judgment He has decided not to."

Jonah was struggling to understand everything. He felt safe just being with this man, but he didn't like the idea that something was coming. He already knew this, though. He'd felt it ever since their last meeting on the beach.

"It time to go now," the man said, turning Jonah around to face the brush again. "I believe it's that way."

"Who are you?" Jonah asked as he turned back toward the test.

"I think you already know," said the man, and then he vanished from view completely.

Jonah shook his head in wonder. But then his mind clicked back in step with the competition, and he wondered if it was true that he really hadn't lost time. Where were the others in the race now? He had no idea how long he'd been in this jungle. Dreams of a victory march to the flagpole were fading fast.

But at least he knew what direction he was supposed to go now.

TWENTY-TWO

THE JUNGLE COMES ALIVE

Jonah moved forward, but his mind was stuck back in the interaction with the man. He felt the peace flow from him again and heard his words, trying to hang on to them and to do what he said. To trust.

Pressing through the jungle as fast as he could, he began to get a feel for the terrain and found himself moving with more confidence. It couldn't be much farther now. He felt like he had moved at least the length of an entire football field, and hopefully farther.

Jonah felt the ground change underneath his feet, and although he hadn't noticed the drop in the landscape from where he had stood on the ridge, he realized he was moving down. Gradually at first, but then steeper down, and it grew even darker. The trees he had seen from up above had all stopped at the same height. But these trees, with branches shooting off in every twisted direction, grew deep down into the forest.

There was no choice. No other route to take. If he was going to get to the other side, he would have to continue downward.

The air cooled dramatically, and he felt a wet chill in his bones as he continued the descent. It appeared as if the entire jungle floor dropped down into blackness. Trees shot up from below, though, and Jonah had no choice but to lower himself down on one of the larger vines hanging off a tree limb.

Okay, Elohim. I'm supposed to trust You. Well, here we go.

He let himself down as quickly as he dared, in near-total darkness. He kept going, farther and farther, wondering if he was going to have to climb back out hand over hand on the other side of this chasm.

His feet squished as he hit the wet ground. Although it was wet, it was flat, and he was able to walk, but he could barely see his hand in front of him. He held his arms out, zombie-like, to try to make sure he didn't run into anything. Suddenly, he had the urge to turn backward and try to climb back up. But he quickly realized that he was here now. The only way to go was forward, through this darkness.

Suddenly, he heard a sound that stopped him in his tracks. It sounded like the noise his bicycle tires made when they were leaking air. A hiss. It went on for a few seconds, then stopped.

Jonah waited, holding his breath, to see if he could hear it again. As he was about to take another step forward, it started once more. Another hiss. It sounded like it was coming from ground level, but he couldn't see anything around him. This time, though, it was louder, as if a half dozen tires were leaking all at once.

He needed to be able to see. Grabbing at his side, he pulled his angelblade out. It cast a white light all around him.

At first, it seemed as if the ground were moving. A sense of cold horror moved up through Jonah's feet, into his legs and the rest of his body as he realized that, of course, the ground itself wasn't moving.

The rain forest floor was covered with snakes.

Jonah held his sword in front of him and spun around, trying to find a path around them. But they were encircling him.

There must have been hundreds, so many that he couldn't see the dirt underneath them. They were slithering across one another, and they all looked the same—black, long, and some with their mouths open so he could see their sharp fangs. Most were curled and twisted, but he saw one stretched out that was longer than he was tall. Their scaly heads were triangular in shape, and he knew from science class that this meant they were very, very venomous.

He hated touching snakes, even at the history and science museum back in Peacefield. When they brought out the snakes— and they only showed kids the ones the workers promised were safe—he would always hang in the back of the group and stuff his hands in his pockets.

He gripped his sword tight and continued to spin in a circle, aware of the snakes that were behind him. Even worse, it appeared that more were emerging from the forest.

"Are these even real?" he wondered out loud, thinking about the competition, with the fake fallen angels and arrows that didn't disintegrate their target. But he remembered the pain he had felt in his shoulder and leg from the arrows that hit him earlier, even if they hadn't left a mark.

He heard a louder hiss behind him and felt his jeans snag and pull hard.

"Oh man!"

Spinning around, he swung his blade close to the ground, slicing through a snake that was rearing back. Its head landed on top of the other snakes, and he saw blood. Reaching down, he felt a hole in his jeans. They were real, all right.

And they seemed to be getting angrier. They were circling him, tangled up and swarming over one another. At least five were rearing back, lifted off the ground and in attack position.

"Aaahhh!" Jonah cried out as he swung his sword around in a circle. It met the heads of the snakes, sending them to their death. But others popped up immediately in their place.

He swung again, with the same result. And once again, more snakes rose and bared their fangs at him, hissing and flicking their forked tongues. They seemed hungry, ready for a bite of human flesh and to sink their poison into his skin. Jonah began to wonder how long he could survive with a snakebite. But he wasn't about to have just one snakebite—he could have a hundred within a matter of minutes.

Could he make a run for it? He wondered if he could get through the snakes, running over the top of them, before they could sink their fangs into him. But how far did they go into the darkness? The hissing was so loud that he couldn't hear anything else. Some of them were attacking each other, they were so thirsty for blood.

He held his sword up higher, and something above caught his eye. A vine hanging down from one of the trees, high above, and out over the swirling snakes. Jonah glanced back down, waving his sword in the faces of those that were getting ready to attack him again. The vine was an almost impossible distance away. It seemed higher to him than the basketball goal back at the convent.

"Think, Jonah, think!" he prodded himself. But if there was another option, it wasn't coming to him.

He took a deep breath, eyeing the vine again while maintaining a watch on the snakes. They were inching closer, and he was quickly running out of time.

Come on, Jonah, you can do this.

He shifted the sword to his left hand and swallowed hard. Bending his knees, he pushed off the ground with as much angel-powered force as he could muster.

He snagged the bottom of the vine with three fingers and prayed that it wouldn't break and send him into the snakes below. Somehow, it was holding!

He held on with one hand, swinging slightly from the jump as the snakes rushed over underneath him. They were snarling, hissing, and mad.

Jonah looked upward, knowing that he needed to climb, and fast. He didn't want to extinguish his blade, but he needed his other hand. Shoving the sword against his side, it disappeared, and the forest went dark again.

He tried to force the hissing noises out of his head as he reached upward. Hand over hand, he climbed until he had a better grasp of the rope and until he felt that he was out of reach of the snakes.

Pulling out his sword again, he realized he was mistaken.

"Oh boy," he muttered.

The snakes were rising along with him. Climbing, one on top of another, they were making a snake-built pyramid.

Soon, they would be at his feet.

Jonah began to swing, back and forth, back and forth. A little at a time at first. Kicking his legs, he began to move faster and faster. He swung over the snakes, now having to lift up his legs to stay out of reach of the highest snake.

Okay, Jonah, it's now or never!

One more big swing.

Then he let go of the rope.

TWENTY-THREE

CAMPFIRE CONVERSATION

He landed just past the last of the snakes, rolling onto the ground. A snake charged toward his face, but he rolled away. Hopping up, Jonah took his sword in his hands again and held it above him like a torch, running into the darkness.

He bounded through a creek, over brush and rocks, weaving through trees as fast as he could. Finally, he stopped and dared to look behind him. There were no snakes in sight. Leaning against a tree, he sucked air in and out for a while, catching his breath.

He wondered if Eliza and Jeremiah had to face snakes today too. Eliza hated them worse than he did. He hoped she didn't have to. Nathaniel had said they would each face tests specific to them. Testing all of their skills, and then some. He tried to brace himself for anything as he moved through the forest.

The ground cover grew dense up ahead, and Jonah pushed through it to find himself standing in a small, circular clearing. He was still surrounded by trees, but the round area he was in was flat and open. Attached to their black, gnarled trunks were lit torches. Their flames danced and cast long, flickering shadows in every direction.

"This is creepy," Jonah said, pointing his sword out in front of him, trying to be ready for anything.

Movement in the trees caught his eyes, and he stiffened. He heard rustling and the sound of branches snapping. Someone— or something—was coming into the circle.

A tall man with a sword emerged from the woods. His golden breastplate shone against dark skin; his arms rippled with muscles as he tossed his blade from one hand to the next. The sword was curved with a sharp hook at the tip and looked appropriate for taking down Philistine soldiers, felling oak trees, or whatever else he needed to do. The man wore the clothes of a Roman soldier, but he seemed not so much like a soldier as a gladiator.

This guy looks like he belongs in the Coliseum, Jonah thought.

The swordsman leaned his bald head back and roared into the air, a war cry that caused Jonah's hands to start trembling. He began moving toward Jonah, his sword raised.

It's only a test, remember, Jonah? As much as he tried to convince himself of that, though, this suddenly felt very, very real. But he knew that if he was going to get to the flag, he was going to have to get past this guy first.

Help me do this, Elohim, he prayed.

The man charged at Jonah with the golden blade out. Jonah steadied himself, ready for the attack, and raised his sword. The man swung down hard, a blow that Jonah met with his glowing angelblade, but that also sent him down to his knees.

Quickly, Jonah pushed himself back up and countered the man's strike with one of his own. Soon, they were going back and forth across the dirt, blades clashing against each other. Jonah managed to block every one of the man's challenges, but he couldn't seem to land any of his own.

The swordsman attacked again, and as Jonah was blocking him, the man pressed himself low to the ground and swung his foot around. It met Jonah's ankle, causing him to slam down to the ground, flat on his back. He raised his golden blade again, and in a flash, brought it down hard.

Shrrrinng! The sound of metal on rock echoed through the woods. Jonah had just managed to roll away, and the sword connected with the dirt and stone beneath him. He kept rolling along the ground as the man continued to swing at him and miss.

Jonah had to do something better than this or he wasn't going to last much longer. This gladiator, or whoever he was, was strong, fast, and relentless, and if he didn't do something fast, getting to the finish line of this race was going to be the least of his concerns.

He summoned all the angel strength he had and pushed back up off the ground, using his blade to block a sword blow at the same time. It was time for Jonah to bring the attack to him.

He began to swing the angelblade furiously, catching the swordsman off guard and pushing him back. The man's arrogant smile had begun to fade now. Jonah saw he was gaining an advantage and pressed even harder. The man was growing tired and was putting all of his energy into blocking Jonah's advances now, not even taking any swings of his own.

Jonah locked swords with the man on the ground, twisted his own blade sharply, and wrenched the golden sword away from his grasp. It went sailing away, clanging against a tree as it flew into the woods. Jonah raised his blade and brought it down as hard as he could. As it met his shoulder, the man disappeared, evaporating into nothing.

Jonah stood for a minute, hands on his knees, resting. He couldn't afford to spend too much time there, though. He already sensed that he was behind. Walking to the edge of the trees, he pushed some branches aside and moved back into the thickness of the forest.

He could tell he was moving even lower, into the bottoms of the woods. The air was cooler and quite thick. He shivered, growing suddenly damp and cold. Moving at a slower pace, he kept a paranoid eye out for more movement in front of him or on the ground. But it was a flickering light ahead that caught his attention.

It wasn't sunlight. It was more like the light of a fire. And it was coming from a hollow in the side of the hill.

Working his way from one tree to the next, Jonah drew closer to the light. He made his way to the front of the cave. The light flickering in the darkness was drawing him in. The entrance was so low that he had to lean over to see inside.

A campfire crackled in the middle of a small, open space on top of a stone floor. Jonah leaned down, mesmerized by the flames, and stepped into the cave.

There were two sawed-off pieces of tree trunk there by the fire, like two chairs awaiting their guests.

In spite of the fire, Jonah felt a coldness worm its way underneath his skin. He suddenly wondered why he was there, why he had stepped into this place. He had to leave. Now. He turned to go, but a voice made his feet freeze.

"Don't leave so soon, Jonah . . . We haven't had a chance to talk in quite some time."

Turning to look deeper into the cave, he saw a figure emerge.

It was a voice he had never forgotten. One he had heard just over a year ago. Not to mention in his worst nightmares. He could only mutter one word.

"You?"

Abaddon stepped forward, the firelight dancing along the sharp curvature of his bony face. His hood covered the rest of his head. He held up a skeleton-like hand.

"Yes, it's me," he said, grinning. "Abaddon, in the flesh. Tell me, how did you like the vipers? I've always had a thing for those creatures."

Jonah tried to gather his wits, but how was that supposed to happen in the presence of the Evil One himself? The one who had led one-third of the angels of heaven into rebellion against Elohim, and ever since had led the charge against the forces of good?

"They were no big deal," he said unconvincingly.

Abaddon laughed. "Well, you made it here, didn't you? So kudos to you!"

Jonah felt his anger well up inside and, in spite of his shaking hands, produced an arrow as fast as he could and aimed it at him.

"Now, Jonah, haven't we done this before?"

Abaddon made a twisting motion with his fingers, and the flame on the tip of Jonah's arrow was doused.

Jonah backed himself slowly toward the cave entrance. His head began to pound even louder than before, and he was starting to feel disoriented. "I think I . . . need to leave now . . ."

Abaddon stepped toward him and spoke in a soothing voice. "You can't leave so soon, Jonah. We've barely had a chance to talk."

Why would I want to have a conversation with the Lord of Darkness himself? He moved another step closer to the entrance and was thinking about making a run for it.

"I am not here to fight with you," he said, placing his forefingers underneath his chin as he walked around the fire. "Don't you want to know, Jonah?"

Jonah blinked. "Know what?"

"Know what the point of all of this has been?" He pointed to Jonah's scarred arms and face. "And your fall, not to mention . . . Eleanor." Abaddon sighed, as if he were deeply sorry about all of it.

The mention of his mother's name caused Jonah to bristle again, and in anger he reached for his angelblade. "I already know what's going on," he seethed. "You, and M'chala, are doing bad things to me and my family!"

Abaddon touched his chin with both forefingers, watching Jonah with his red eyes. Jonah tried to look away from them. "Yes, but don't you want to know . . . why?"

Jonah paused, entranced by the question. So much of him wanted to leave, but a bigger part needed to know the answer. His hesitation gave Abaddon the chance to beckon him back into the cave. Jonah felt his feet moving toward the fire again. He sat down on one of the tree stumps.

"Watch carefully, young quarterling," cooed Abaddon. He waved his hand in front of the fire, and it began to morph. Flames gradually began to take shape. Jonah gasped as he looked deeper in, focusing all of his attention on the unfolding scene in front of him.

Abaddon nodded his head as the scene came into view clearly.

It was a picture of a darkened hallway, and in it, a hazy green being floating along. Jonah recognized it instantly.

M'chala.

He stopped at one of the rooms and slid under the crack. Jonah could see inside the room now too, and instantly he knew it to be his own. The view was from above, and he saw David sleeping on one side. M'chala stood over him for a minute, as if contemplating what horrible disease he could give his friend. Then he moved over to the other bed. Jonah knew that he was watching an image of himself, sleeping.

Jonah gasped as he watched M'chala press his finger into his chest, twisting and turning it with enthusiasm. In a few seconds, he was finished, and he slid from the room.

The image died in the fire. But just as quickly, another appeared. Jonah was in a different hallway, another one he was familiar with. He brought his hand up to his mouth as he recognized the faded, tan carpet.

It was his old house in Peacefield.

M'chala was there too, a haze of green, floating along, until he turned into a room on the left.

"No," Jonah whispered, even though he knew he was watching something that had already taken place.

M'chala stood over his mom and dad, savoring the moment. Then, in a similar way, he plunged his fist down into Eleanor's body.

She trembled and her body rose, almost floating out of the bed. Benjamin stirred but didn't wake up. Jonah could see the pain twisting her face, but her eyes stayed closed. Soon, M'chala was finished, and he glided out of the room.

"Why?" he whispered. "Why would you do that to us?"

But the scene in front of him changed yet again. This time it was of a great hall, full of people. As it zoomed in, Jonah realized they were angels.

They stood together, speaking to one another in small, scattered groups. The scene was blurry around the edges, so Jonah couldn't make out much about the place. But it was bright and felt majestic.

He studied the angels below him, and one caught his attention. She had silver hair, beautiful wings almost the same color, and a light blue robe. *Is that Camilla?*

Suddenly the angels split in half, making room for someone coming into the room. A dark, hooded creature strolled through. *Abaddon!* Jonah felt his chest tighten at the sight of the Evil One. His presence apparently surprised the angels too.

It was as if Jonah was floating over him as he walked forward, heading toward a set of doors at the end of the aisle. They opened, and Abaddon disappeared into the next room.

Jonah kept floating over, and then he saw Abaddon again, walking by himself along a simple pathway, moving more and more into the light. He removed his hood and bent down on one knee. Then he stood again. He began to speak, and although Jonah couldn't see who he was speaking to, he already knew.

He's speaking to Elohim!

Abaddon was talking, then listening, and then speaking some more, but Jonah was unable to hear the conversation. It was as if it were on mute. But then, someone must have turned the sound on, because he could suddenly hear.

"Why shouldn't you be proud of the resilience of your people?" Abaddon said with an aura of wickedness betraying his smile. "They are very well protected by Your angels."

Elohim must have spoken then, but Jonah could only hear Abaddon's responses.

"What about these quarterlings, the outcast children of the

monster nephilim?" Abaddon seethed. "They seem to be especially well guarded. This boy, Jonah Stone, and the rest of them . . . they can do no wrong."

Abaddon listened again, and Jonah noticed that the Evil One was unable, or unwilling, to look at Elohim directly. Even the prince of darkness was humbled in the presence of God.

"Give him over to me," Abaddon murmured. "This faith You speak of—maybe it's not so strong after all. If You would only loosen Your protection of him, we can see how faithful he really is."

He listened to more words from Elohim, then bowed low.

"Yes, of course. His life remains in Your hands," he said. "But by Your permission, other things . . . and other people around him . . . are fair game."

He turned and walked back to the doorway, his head still bowed low.

Jonah closed his eyes, feeling the words from the Evil One sink into his heart, confirming his worst fears. He had been singled out for an attack. And for some reason, Elohim was allowing it to happen. And what was worse, others around him had been affected too.

The scene faded away, turning back to flames whipping against each other in the cave. Jonah sat, stunned, blinking at the fire.

"Now, don't you see who is really responsible for all of this?" Abaddon said, pacing behind Jonah, his smooth voice purring in his ears. "He summoned me to His throne. He put you in harm's way. And not only you, but also your friends and your family. It was Elohim, don't you see?" His voice began to grow louder with each word. "This is all . . . *His* . . . *FAULT*!"

Jonah shoved his hands on his ears, but Abaddon's screeching voice was inside his head already. He jumped up from the tree stump and bolted through the cave entrance and back out into the woods.

TWENTY-FOUR

THE FLAGPOLE

A baddon didn't pursue him from the cave, but he was laughing, and Jonah needed to do anything he could to get away from his voice. It echoed through the forest. He couldn't get away from it fast enough.

He finally slowed down enough to begin to put thoughts together that made sense. The scene the Evil One had shown him raced through his mind again. Abaddon, splitting the middle of the band of angels; the shocked looks on their faces; and then Abaddon, summoned to appear in front of Elohim.

And then, the unbelievable . . . Elohim giving him permission to attack Jonah and his family? Was Abaddon right? Was this really all His fault? The very idea of it hit Jonah in the stomach and almost took his breath away.

But it was Abaddon . . . nothing he said could be trusted. The images, though, and the conversation—it all looked so real. Could he have just made it up? Some elaborate trick he was playing on Jonah's mind?

He didn't know what to think. His head spun, his thoughts tying themselves into knots that he was having a hard time untangling. He found himself slowing down to a slow run, and then a walk. Then he just stopped and stood.

With a thud on the forest floor, he landed on his knees.

He had no idea how long he had been on the ground when he heard the words, tumbling down to the forest floor like autumn leaves let go in the wind.

The Lord is my shepherd, I lack nothing.

Jonah opened his eyes, feeling his face against moss and dirt.

He makes me lie down in green pastures, he leads me beside quiet waters, he refreshes my soul.

It was the voice of Camilla, his old friend, the angel, speaking the psalm to him. He looked around, trying to see if she was near.

He guides me along the right paths for his name's sake.

Jonah pushed himself up, the cave a farther distance away now, both in the forest and in his mind. With each word, he felt the power of Abaddon retreat a little more.

Even though I walk through the darkest valley, I will fear no evil, for you are with me; your rod and your staff, they comfort me.

The words felt like life to him, flowing into his body and giving him strength. Jonah found his determination once again. He pushed off the floor, his legs feeling stronger now. The boils were still there, painful as ever, but he ignored them for now. The words were filling him up, and somehow, in the middle of the darkness around him, with the weight of Abaddon's words, he felt as if he had just enough power to finish the journey.

A singular shaft of light broke through the dense branches in front of him, and he knew which direction to go.

Jonah knew he had probably failed the exam, but that was

the least of his worries right now. He needed to get out of this awful forest, find the finish line, and, more importantly, find the quarterlings, his parents, and the angels. At this point, he was actually surprised he was getting out of here alive.

The sun broke through again, and as he brushed past beautiful white and lavender flowers climbing up a vine wrapped around a tree, he wondered how he could have descended into that awful pit while in a place so pretty.

He heard what sounded like people cheering from a long way off before he saw anything. The farther along he moved, the louder it became.

It's coming from the stands, he remembered. *The parents in those bleachers surrounding the flagpole. They're probably awarding Frederick the grand prize already.*

Jonah felt his heart sink a little, but he ran forward anyway, pushing through the forest as fast as he could. He came to the center of the rain forest, which opened up into a circular clearing. The stands were in front of him, and he could see the colorful flag flapping up above.

There was no doubt. They were cheering. *They must be cheering for all of the quarterlings already there. There's no way I am anything but last.*

He jogged down the narrow dirt path in between two sets of bleachers and looked up, shielding his eyes from the suddenly hot Hawaiian sun. It had been so dark inside the pit that it took his eyes a few seconds to adjust. The crowd's cheering grew louder as Jonah emerged, and those who were close to the course leaned over the sides of the bleachers, pointing at him and clapping wildly.

Jonah's eyes were drawn to a set of large screens, positioned all around the makeshift stadium. His face was currently on all of them, a close-up. His mouth dropped slightly at the image. He saw the confusion, weariness, and surprise on his own face.

And underneath his face, two words:

FIRST PLACE

He looked toward the flagpole and saw there was no one around it. How could that be? He had been in there for what felt like hours. Maybe even a half day.

But it was clear from the cheering that he was, indeed, in first place.

Jonah began running faster toward the flagpole now, more energized than he had been in hours.

Another cheer erupted, and the screens quickly shifted to another face. A handsome, tan, blond-haired head filled the space. Frederick was running opposite Jonah, looking as bewildered as Jonah did, but running faster.

The flagpole stood in between them.

And something inside of Jonah clicked.

He began to push himself and soon found his sandals of speed. He could tell from the dust Frederick was kicking up that he must have found his too.

Jonah was almost there, but so was Frederick. He thought about all the events Frederick had won and how much he had struggled with everything lately. And then, he decided that none of it mattered anymore.

All that mattered was what was happening right now.

And right now, Jonah was determined that he was going to win.

He rushed toward the pole, bearing down, almost there. He didn't want to even look at Frederick, because he knew he was pushing just as hard.

Come on, Jonah! COME ON!

Slap!

Jonah's hand hit the pole.

Slap!

Less than a second later, Frederick's hand landed on his.

Jonah had won.

The crowd of parents roared their approval, and Jonah suddenly grabbed Frederick and hugged him tight.

"Are you okay?" he said into his ear. He knew in his heart that Frederick, and every other quarterling, had gone through the same thing he just had.

Frederick hugged him back, Jonah feeling him shake slightly. "Yeah, I'm all right. It was crazy, though."

"Yeah, no kidding," Jonah answered, wondering if they had experienced the same thing. A question for later. "Eliza, Jeremiah . . . have you seen them?"

Frederick looked at him blankly and shook his head. "No, no, I haven't. I didn't see any of the quarterlings. But it looks like from that video screen, we're getting ready to see them now."

Jonah heard the cheering grow once again. He looked up at the screen to see the faces of Eliza and then Jeremiah filling it up.

Frederick slapped Jonah on the back and laughed.

The two came running from different sides of the clearing, meeting in the middle to touch the flagpole.

"Are you guys okay?" Jonah said to them both. "How did you do with the snakes? That gladiator guy with the sword? And what about Abaddon?"

Eliza looked at him, tilting her head to the side. "Abaddon?" she said. "Didn't see him back there, thank goodness. But I saw some other awful stuff, good grief." She was about to launch into the tale of what happened to her, but then he turned to his younger brother.

"Did you?" Jonah asked. "Any of that . . . ?"

Jeremiah looked at Eliza, shrugging his shoulders, then back to Jonah. "I didn't see anything like that out there either—just some monsters that I had to deal with. It got pretty crazy for a while," he said. Then he brushed a speck of dirt off his shoulder. "But I took care of business, of course. No problem."

Eliza and Frederick burst out laughing. Jonah couldn't help but smile as his brother began to act out the fight he'd apparently had with some kind of large monster in the woods.

Soon they were joined, one by one, by the rest of the quarterlings making it through the rain forest, sharing their own stories, each one unique.

Rupert, who had his own story to tell, had also been listening to the others. "I guess we all had to face some things we are pretty afraid of," he said, his normal scowl at least temporarily gone. "What about you there, Jonah?"

The quarterlings turned toward him, expecting a similar story.

"Some other time," replied Jonah. He didn't feel like discussing it right now. Too many emotions were swirling around.

Nathaniel, Camilla, Marcus, and Taryn, with wings spread wide, floated down in front of the quarterlings.

"Excellent work today, students! Beautiful," Camilla said, her blue eyes shining bright.

Nathaniel nodded, his hands clasped behind his back. "Terrific job today, my friends. Very impressive."

"I agree," came the voice of another angel, soaring over their heads. The Archangel Michael touched down beside Nathaniel and Camilla. They bowed their heads in deference to him. He stood in front of the quarterlings, nodding his approval. "You did very well today, quarterlings. And some of you showed extraordinary courage in the face of an extreme challenge. You are to be commended."

The quarterlings gathered around, in awe of the powerful presence of the commanding angel. He stood before them unsmiling, but his eyes were bright and filled with love for them.

Nathaniel handed him a piece of paper. "And now, it is my honor to announce the final scores for your midterm examinations for Angel School."

Jonah turned toward Frederick, getting ready to extend his hand in congratulations for a job well done. He was sure that, even with his victory, there was no way he had actually won the competition.

Michael studied the page for a few seconds, a small smile now brightening his face. "In a very close battle, the top of the class goes to . . . Jonah Stone!"

His mouth dropped, and he looked at Frederick, expecting to see a scowl. Instead, Frederick was clapping and cheering with the rest. Jonah felt his face grow hot, but he couldn't stop grinning.

He stepped forward, bowing his head toward Michael and leaning down as Nathaniel placed a shiny golden medal around his neck.

"Nice job, Jonah," Eliza said, smiling, as he stood beside her.

"Not so bad yourself," said Jonah, putting his arm around her shoulder.

The quarterlings crowded around him, but the only thing Jonah wanted to do was see his mom and dad.

The silhouette of his mother caught his eye, emerging from a group of the parents. Usually she stood tall, but she was hunched over, and Jonah could tell with one look that she was still very, very sick. Beside her, the shorter, rounder outline of his father came into view. He was holding her elbow as they walked slowly toward him.

He couldn't remember ever being so glad to see his parents. He walked briskly toward them, wanting to share everything with them about what he'd seen in the woods. Maybe now they could figure out how to defeat M'chala and send him away from them for good.

"Mom! Dad!" he called out, concern building in him more and more the closer he grew to his mother.

"Jonah!" his dad said. "Awesome job today! Incredible. We got to watch some of it on the screens, except for when you went into that cave. What happened in there?"

His mother looked at him with tears in her green eyes and spoke in a weak voice. "Wonderful, dear. Brilliant. You made it through. Your father and I are so, so proud of you."

Jonah barely noticed the angels floating around back and forth above them. He was only about ten feet apart from his parents when an angel swooped down and landed in between Eleanor and Benjamin.

"Uh, hi there," Benjamin said, a little uncomfortable with how close the gleaming angel was.

The angel said nothing but reached down and grabbed Eleanor's wrist. At the same time, he pushed Benjamin down to the ground.

A flurry of activity was suddenly in the air around them. Jonah heard a scream and then the loud voice of Michael commanding something that he couldn't make out, and felt people rushing in their direction.

"Say good-bye, Jonah," the angel hissed.

Everything from that point on happened in slow motion. He looked at his mother and then into the face of the angel.

The fallen angel.

Just before he transported, the creature morphed into its true self, black, crusty, and dark.

And then, with a snap, Eleanor and the angel vanished.

TWENTY-FIVE

SHADOWS CAST

Jonah ran over to where his mom was only seconds earlier. He spun around, looking everywhere. His dad was still on the ground, staring up. Angels were around him, barking commands, moving in every direction. Eliza came running up, with Jeremiah behind her.

"Where's Mom? What happened?" Jeremiah was asking questions that no one was able to answer.

"It was a messenger angel," Jonah said. "A fallen one . . . It took her before we could do anything."

Things were swirling around him. Michael was sending angels this direction and that, some already communicating to others via Angelic Vortex.

The archangel came running over to the Stone family. "We're doing everything we can to find her right now."

"I know. Please hurry," Benjamin said, standing up, looking disoriented.

"Mom!" Jonah called out, turning around in a circle. "Mom!"

He knew there would be no answer. A messenger angel had taken her. There was no telling where she was now.

"Can't you track a messenger angel?" Eliza asked Michael.

He shook his head. "I'm afraid that they are completely untraceable. Even to us."

As they were standing there, an image formed on the screens still on display from the exams.

It was a fuzzy picture of his mother.

"Mom!" he yelled. But she couldn't hear him. She was somewhere else, and even though the image grew clearer, the dark surroundings gave him no clue as to where she might be.

"There she is!" Jeremiah cried out. "Who has her there?"

They were completely helpless. All of them, even the angels. Even Michael. They moved toward the screen, but there was nothing they could do. All they could do was watch.

She was being held by two fallen angels, and she wasn't struggling very much. Jonah's heart hit his throat when the slithery M'chala crept into view.

"Mom, watch out!" he yelled, even though he knew his words were futile.

M'chala turned around, though, and looked directly at Jonah.

He held his finger over Eleanor, who pulled against the angels as they braced themselves to restrain her. She may have been sick, but she was still a nephilim.

M'chala placed his other hand on her shoulder to steady her and drove his finger into her chest.

Her eyes fluttered once, then opened, looking straight at them all. He thought for a brief second that she may even say something, but then her eyes shut again.

By the limpness of her body, Jonah knew that she was gone.

∞

Jonah sat in the dirt beside Eliza and Jeremiah. He ran his hand into the dirt until it was just as black. The picture up above had disappeared some time ago. There were hushed conversations going on all around them, but it was awkwardly quiet. Quarterlings, nephilim, and angels formed a sort of circle around them, trying to figure out what to do, making plans, but they were giving the Stone kids their space.

Jonah half expected a fallen angel to come and attack them now that they were already down. Maybe M'chala would come for him too.

Whatever. He didn't care.

Finally, he rose, unable to even feel his legs, or anything else, for that matter. He stumbled through the crowd, his eyes searching, people offering soft "I'm so sorry's" and other kind words he barely heard.

He found his dad, who was standing with Camilla, her hand on his arm.

"Dad?"

His eyes met his son's, and Jonah saw them melt. He fell into his dad's shoulder, and they both wept.

TWENTY-SIX

SNOWFALL

From his seat on the train, Jonah stared out at the landscape moving by. The mounds of dirty snow were the same charcoal gray as most of the buildings he passed. He held his hand up, lazily tracing the outline of an angel in the moisture on the window. His hand was unscarred now, just like the rest of his body. Immediately after his mother died, the boils all over had disappeared, although it took Eliza pointing it out for him to even notice. His headaches were gone too. But it was nothing he felt like celebrating in the face of losing her.

Winter had set in four weeks ago, just after his mother's funeral in Peacefield, and the first storm of the season rolled in, dumping two feet of snow on their sleepy town. Usually, the first snow of the year was like a sugar high for the Stone kids, injecting them with an extra dose of energy that could be spent only by afternoons of sledding and snowball fights.

But their house had been subdued and all too quiet, to the point that it began to drive Jonah outside. He'd do anything to get away from the silent, empty rooms and the feelings he was having. He would wake up and walk into the kitchen, somehow expecting her to be there, whipping up an amazing breakfast, hands moving in a thousand directions at once. And then he would realize, again, that she wasn't.

He didn't join in with the other kids on their street, screaming and shouting and laughing in the snow. He found himself instead taking long walks. Sometimes Eliza or Jeremiah would join him. Other times, he would go alone.

∾

It was on his walk last night that Jonah decided he would come to New York again. His father could give him answers, thoughts, and theories. But he needed more than that. He needed to talk to someone who knew.

"Jonah Stone!" Camilla said, looking up from a stack of notes on her desk. "I wondered when I might see you. What a wonderful surprise."

She rose and gave him a big hug, then stood in front of him, sizing him up for a few seconds.

"We've missed you around here," she said. "All of you. Angel School has continued, but it hasn't been the same without the Stone kids. How is everyone holding up?"

Jonah shrugged, picking up a paperweight from her desk and studying it. "Everyone's doing all right, I guess. It's been . . . hard."

She nodded, her eyes welling up as she sat back down. "And you would like some answers."

He looked up, meeting her eyes with his, and unable to hide the fire in them. "Yeah. Don't you think I deserve some?"

She motioned to the chair to his right, and he sat down. Leaning back in hers, she pivoted, looking through the window at the snow. It was beginning to fall again.

"I know you want answers, Jonah. Why M'chala targeted you. Why Elohim allowed it. Why your mother is gone." She paused, not moving too quickly past the weight of those words. "But sometimes, even the angels are prevented from understanding His mystery."

"Why did He make this happen?" Jonah exploded, his face reddening, and he felt himself lose control more than he intended. It was a question—*the question*—he had been turning over and over again.

Camilla turned and faced him squarely. "Of course He didn't make this happen, Jonah! Don't you know better than that at this point? After all you have been through, after everything He has shown you, done for you, and led you through. Do you really believe He would cause awful things to happen to you and to those you love?"

Jonah folded his arms, slumping into his chair a little more. He knew her words rang true somewhere in his heart, but he wasn't ready to back off just yet. "He let it happen, didn't He?"

Camilla smiled at him sadly. "Yes, He did."

"So what does that mean?" Jonah asked, still smoldering. "What does that say about Him? Why would Elohim let Abaddon have his way with me?"

"You are not the first to be tested in this way, Jonah," she said. "Many other followers before you have been allowed to experience dire situations, attack, and, yes, even death by Abaddon's forces. It is a mark of honor and should be taken as such."

Jonah turned back toward her, her words causing him to boil again. "Honor? Really? The fallen angel of disease targeted me . . .

and my friends and family . . . all because Elohim chose to let it happen . . . and this is some kind of honor?"

Camilla sat up straight and leaned forward. "Jonah, the loss of Eleanor was a great loss to all of us. To me. And my loss is nothing compared to yours and that of your father, brother, and sister. But it is an honor to be tested in this way. Many do not see it that way, but it is absolutely correct. Elohim has His plan, and you can be assured that He has something in mind with all of this. He has never once let you, or your family, or even your mother, out of His grasp."

She arose and moved over to the chair beside Jonah now.

"You are to grieve this loss, yes. And it's even all right to be angry. But do not let it cause you to hide—especially not from Him. There is a difference."

Jonah sat still, trying to keep his lip from trembling. He realized that for a month he had been doing that, trying not to break down, to stay strong, to do whatever it was he thought he was supposed to do. But in the safety of her office, he felt the wall inside begin to crumble.

His shoulders began to shake, softly at first, then progressively harder. His first instinct was to cover his face with his hands as the tears began to fall, even though it was only Camilla. Thoughts began to run wild. Memories of his mom came quickly, her smiling face, that time when she dropped a carton of eggs on the kitchen floor, another time when they snuggled together on the sofa and watched a movie. And more. Pain like a knife cut through his chest, and his lungs began to heave in and out as his entire body shook. He had no control of himself, and the waves crashed over him.

He felt a gentle hand on his shoulder, rubbing his arm softly.

Camilla said nothing, allowing the waves of grief to come, praying silently for him.

A word came to him from somewhere deep within, rising up, bubbling from a place tucked down in some crease in his soul. It moved through his stomach, rose into his throat and mouth. It was equal parts cry, declaration, and confession.

"Elohim . . ."

Jonah had no idea how long he sat there, but finally the waves subsided and he was able to breathe normally again. He felt like he'd just run ten wind sprints at basketball practice. Exhaustion was overtaking him. But the waves had been replaced by calmer waters, bringing to him a deep sense of relief.

Camilla sat there, still silent, rubbing the back of his neck with her hand.

Finally, he peeled himself out of the chair, rubbing his face with his hands. "I need to get home before my dad starts to worry about me."

"Should I contact a messenger angel for you?" Camilla asked. Jonah knew it wasn't the normal mode of transportation allowed for the quarterlings. It was a generous offer.

"No, it's okay," he said. "I don't mind riding the subway."

She raised her eyebrows but didn't push.

He turned around before he walked through the door. "Thanks, Camilla. I really mean it. I guess I just needed to get that out."

"You're welcome." Camilla smiled. "Just know that we are all thinking of you often, praying for you, and looking forward to the day when you will be back with us at Angel School. Do you happen to have an idea of when that might be, by the way?"

Jonah hesitated, thinking, his hand on the door handle. "Thanks again, Camilla. For everything."

He walked down to the street, wrapped his scarf snugly around his neck, and shoved his hands deep into his warm coat, leaving behind him new tracks on the fresh, white snow.

∽

Jonah sat with Eliza on his left and Jeremiah on his right, listening to his father speak once again. The pews of the church were full of people, young, old, and in between. They had come from many different places in life, but for one reason—in search of the presence of Elohim. To express what was on their hearts to Him. To remember, once again, that in spite of the battles they were facing, He was in control and He loved them.

The people stood, and Benjamin joined his family in the pew as the guitar strummed the first soft chord. He placed his arm around Jeremiah and winked at Jonah. Jeremiah wrapped both arms around him and squeezed tightly.

Jonah studied the words on the screen and once again thought about his mom. How her voice had sounded when she sang, how her face had looked when she closed her eyes and prayed.

And then something connected, deep within him. A thought he hadn't had until now.

That his mom was with Elohim this very moment, basking in His presence and worshipping.

And so were they. Even though they were here, and she was there, maybe right now, she was singing too, raising her voice once again to the God she had never doubted, always loved, and forever trusted—the God who had forever been faithful to her.

This realization jolted Jonah, and he stood suddenly taller, closing his eyes, lifting up his voice to the heavens. He sang with all of the air his lungs could give and felt the tears begin to wet his cheeks. He pictured his mother singing too, right beside him, and knew that, even in death, the connection he had with her could never be broken.

He joined the rest of the church—and his mom—in heartfelt praise to Elohim.

ABOUT THE AUTHOR

Jerel Law is a gifted communicator and pastor with twenty years of full-time ministry experience. He holds a master of divinity degree from Gordon-Conwell Theological Seminary and began writing fiction as a way to encourage his children's faith to come alive. Law lives in North Carolina with his family. Learn more at www.jerellaw.com.

Travel back in time to London and solve mysteries with Sherlock Holmes's protégé!

Griffin Sharpe notices everything, which makes him the perfect detective! And since he lives next door to Sherlock Holmes, mysteries always seem to find him. With Griffin's keen mind and strong faith, together with his Uncle Rupert's genius inventions, there is no case too tricky for the detectives of 221 Baker Street!

By Jason Lethcoe

www.tommynelson.com
www.jasonlethcoe.com/holmes

Check out all of the great books in the series!

No Place Like Holmes ❖ *The Future Door*

There is an unseen world of good
and evil where nightmares are
fought and hope is reborn.

ENTER THE DOOR WITHIN.

Aidan's life is completely uprooted when his parents
move the family across the country to care for his ailing
grandfather. But when he begins having nightmares and
eerie events occur around his neighborhood, Aidan finds
himself drawn to his grandfather's basement—where he
discovers three ancient scrolls and a mysterious invitation
to another world.

By Wayne Thomas Batson

www.tommynelson.com

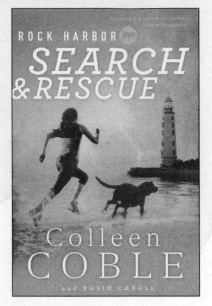

FROM AWARD-WINNING AUTHOR COLLEEN COBLE COMES HER FIRST SERIES FOR YOUNG ADVENTURERS: A MIXTURE OF MYSTERY, SUSPENSE, ACTION—AND ADORABLE PUPPIES!

Eighth-grader Emily O'Reilly is obsessed with all things Search-and-Rescue. The almost-fourteen-year-old spends every spare moment on rescues with her stepmom Naomi and her canine partner Charley. But when an expensive necklace from a renowned jewelry artist is stolen under her care at the fall festival, Emily is determined to prove her innocence to a town that has immediately labeled her guilty.

As Emily sets out to restore her reputation, she isn't prepared for the surprises she and the Search-and-Rescue dogs uncover along the way. Will Emily ever find the real thief?

BY COLLEEN COBLE

www.tommynelson.com
www.colleencoble.com